HOUSE OF OTTER

Claiming
ALEXANDER

HOUSE OF OTTER 1

Claiming ALEXANDER

LEO SPARX

4 HORSEMEN
PUBLICATIONS INC.

Claiming Alexander

Copyright © 2020 Leo Sparx. All rights reserved.

4 Horsemen
Publications, Inc.

4 Horsemen Publications, Inc.
1497 Main St. Suite 169
Dunedin, FL 34698
4horsemenpublications.com
info@4horsemenpublications.com
Cover & Typesetting by Battle Goddess Productions
Editor Nita Edetor

Ebook: 978-1-64450-102-3

Paperback: 978-1-64450-103-0

DEDICATION

TO ALL THE OTTER BOYS
I'VE LOVED BEFORE...

Table of Contents

Chapter One

W e didn't have trees that showed fall colors in
Beachside. On the adjacent stretch of town where
I went to visit them, the sky faded from blue to
grey as I passed by the type of houses I was too poor to live
in. Throughout the length of the day it had been mostly silent
aside from autumn leaves drifting just below the canopy before
settling to the crunchy ground. Here, there were mansions with
enough forest acreage to be called manors and have their own
names, acting as landmarks as I continued on my typical path.
They were all surrounded by walls and pushed back behind iron
gates to keep the common people, like me, out.

I often imagined the people living inside to be their own
particular shade of happiness. Vibrant yellow or burnt orange,
maybe some color yet to be discovered or too expensive for
someone raised where I was to see outside of a museum. The
residents inside made into complete people with polished cars,
extensive closets, and shiny things only real money could buy.
What I experienced on my walks over to the better side of town
seemed to start with loneliness and end with deep longing.

One house, the final exhibit which often ended my tour,
stood as alone as I felt. The dark brick and painted wood framed
in a mist from winter looming in the vegetation. I stood at the

easement of overgrown hedges and moist grass, admiring the tall pillars and variety of shapes creating the massive structure. It was so incredible in size that even merely seeing the front moved me to call it a castle. Not far from where I stood, formed in welded metal letters that were rusting at the edges, the archway above the locked gate read, "The House of Otter."

Running my hands across the brick, it was rough and sandy against the sensitive skin of my fingertips. Something always led me to finish my routine in the wooded area near the end of the wall bordering the property. I'd never understood it, but without fail, at my first glimpse of the building, something would arise in me alongside the melancholy. The general gloom and mystery created a tension between the fabric below my jeans that felt like excitement and begged for instant release.

It had become a ritual, upon seeing the house, to continue to glide my fingers along the length of the wall until it stopped. Then, walk a few paces into the forest until I found a large tree to lean against. The smell of moss and bark filling me as I planted my boots into the soft dirt below, I intended to take my time. To let my thumb and index finger find their way under my t-shirt and around my nipples, leaving my abdomen exposed to the light breeze of the woods while I pinched and swirled around the sensitive skin. The line of hair leading into my jeans, reacting to the air—a direct trail to my growing stiffness—as my nipples formed into cylinders poking through the cotton of my shirt.

By that point, it was all I could do to keep myself from letting at least one hand wander, to tease and play with the top button of my jeans. To let a single finger push its way inside the space between the textile and my skin. The tightness of the stretchy band moving the delicate flesh against my forefinger bone, back and forth, in and out. Begging to be thrust deeper into the warmth building just inches further below.

Spiralling my fingertip against the metal of the clasp, the chill of the round button in the breeze sent a delightful rush through my body, making my nipples and cock even harder. My back against the green moss of the broad tree trunk, I let it carry my weight as I leaned further back to finally release the button and allow my grasp to move to the solidness of the bronze zipper. Flicking it back and forth with care, mimicking the motions I ached to apply to the pulsing bulge underneath; just the thought of rubbing the exposed head of my cock in this way made the tension near unbearable and suddenly I was tugging the zipper downward, the matching teeth opening slowly.

Immediately, the crisp autumn air made the pre-cum dripping from me icy. The droplets dew on a furry meadow, viscous and slippery as I used my palm to coat the length of my thickness with the liquid. The temperatures combined into a sensation so pleasurable, I was producing much more natural lubrication than usual. Enough that I could bring the taste to my bottom lip with a finger to sample the flavor by running my tongue across, before taking a firmer grasp around the girth of myself.

Finally giving myself permission to stroke, I thought about the House of Otter. I imagined the mysterious man inside I had only heard stories about and wondered if he really did have a house full of hairy boys that were his possessions; if there was a chance it could be true once he owned them, they were his forever. The idea of giving myself to someone in that way, trading my body for comfort and security, the pulsing part of me knew for certain: I would give anything to live behind those walls.

To me, the house seemed empty, as I had never on even one of my walks seen anyone coming or going. No cars in the grand driveway or rolling down the long blacktop, no people through the opaque windows. The aged gate remained padlocked shut. Most likely the legends the people on my side of town had created—the stories of this eccentric millionaire—were intended to amuse themselves. There was no man. No collection of boys for him to play with. And yet, the sight of the house had sent me into such a state of arousal I couldn't help but imagine life inside the manor.

It was often paired with that thought that I could feel everything building inside me, everything contracting and ready to release. Looking down at my cock, the pubic hair surrounding the mound, dense and slightly curled—I thought of the past, about the boys who had complimented my size. While I appreciated their admiration, and at certain points their hands and mouths, it had never been more than physical, rarely anything other than a form of quick release. As time passed, I'd discovered nothing was as satisfying as my walks in the woods, alone with my own inner palm and fantasies of the house.

My mouth facing the momentum of my hand stroking continuously, I parted my lips and let my tongue push forth enough saliva to further lubricate. The new liquid created a silky glide that found its way into the foreskin surrounding my bare head. From the base of my pubic bone to my exposed peak, the spit slid back and forth between the wet cock-sized hole I'd formed with my fist. Pulling the loosened foreskin over and around the head sent me into a trance that forced me to lose my balance. My boots slipped in the soggy dirt below while my hard cock stood out in the open space and my balls hung through my parted jeans.

Steadying myself, sweat starting to form in the thick hair under my armpits, I moved the hand that had been keeping attention to my nipples to the bottom of my shirt and quickly tucked the material into my mouth. It was doubtful anyone could hear me out this far into the woods, and regardless of the stories I had created in my mind—the ones sending me over the edge—there was probably not a soul dwelling in the adjacent manor. But still, stuffing the base of my sweat-covered shirt in my mouth would give me more access to vigorously stroke as I came and stifle any moans or screams as well.

I thought about a smirking man tracing the salty residue on my abdomen with his tongue. His fingers in my mouth, holding the fabric of my shirt in place, telling me if I were a good boy, I would cum hard. I would shoot my load for him and give him every drop I had inside me. But, I would do it, quietly.

By then it was too much, and I felt everything I held inside of me that day form a crescendo. The grey clouds above and crunching brown leaves below, the sadness I had carried with me the entire walk through the countryside; now lay on the ground near my boots, having burst from me in a series of quick spurts.

The relief was immediate, but temporary. I let the white release settle into the moistened earth as I tucked myself away and re-fastened the zipper to close my jeans. My shirt, dampened from my mouth, now hung slightly misshapen around my waist.

Exhaling, I pushed myself from the tree and let my footing normalize. The weight I had been holding in my planted boots returning to the rest of my body was dizzying, and now the autumn chill was cooling the sweat on the rest of my body.

My walks had become the best part of my day, and now that portion of the day was over. On my way out of the woods and back to my more humble existence, I looked back at the House of Otter. I thought about the man I had conjured in my imagination just moments before, the one whose fingers in my mouth tasted like money and power.

CHAPTER TWO

B ack home, the wooden shutters had been crumbling since before I moved in. No one ever bothered locking the door. Using my evening to walk around the better side of town did little anymore to help me forget that by nightfall I'd be back where rain leaked through the brittle roof and buckets caught the water that eventually spilled over into the stained beige carpet. Tonight—even though it hadn't rained in days—on the couch between two full leak receptacles, the first thing I saw was a backpack.

My eyes adjusted through the dim lighting enough to eventually see that the backpack, though seemingly suspended in mid-air and pumping back and forth, was attached to a male frame. Broad shoulders and buzzed hair, pants pulled down just enough, as if he was making a quick stop at the urinal. In front of him was my roommate Darius, balanced on his knees between the sagging cushions. On all-fours with his elbows over the back of the couch, his furry ass was facing the stranger. Backward hat in position, he was prepared for the moment the boy behind him was ready to shoot his load; assuring the bill wouldn't get in the way of any drops landing in his mouth when he transitioned to face him.

Chapter Two

The sound of the creaking door didn't stop the stranger or my friend. For a quick moment, Darius's brown eyes were on me, the side of his face—stubble and half-smile—pressed on the harder part of the couch, moving in rhythm. He raised his eyebrows, looking down toward the crotch of my jeans with a sparkle in his eye, an invitation. Whether I'd just spent myself out in the woods or not, the answer had always been, and would always be, "No, thank you."

Free sex had never been difficult for me to come by in this house, if I had wanted it. For Darius and the rest of the boys living here, a fee was only required for an outsider. With the amount of patrons coming and going, there was a reason the front door remained unbolted, why the couch and beds were lumpy and always slightly damp in any season. I couldn't judge the other boys in the house. While I didn't partake in the offers for a free hookup with any of them, it wasn't because I thought of them as dirty or damaged; they were all cute in their own way and nice enough. To look down on them would be to paint my own portrait with the same materials. Because there was a reason we all ended up here together, and it involved our shared profession.

Flopping on the bed in my room, I found staring at the ceiling did little to facilitate an escape. The peeling wallpaper and patches of mildew in the corners, the hinges on everything rusting and shedding red-brown dust to the floor were constant reminders that I was living in what barely qualified as a house. Certainly not prestigious enough to have its own laid-brick privacy wall, or tall hedges, and definitely not its own name. Not like the House of Otter.

As empty as I was, I could feel myself getting hard again just thinking about being back in the woods near the manor, about the man who had stifled my screams of ecstasy, my moans of pure pleasure. The idea of him had seemed so real in the woods—his fingers and tongue tracing my sweat and skin, his words in my ear with demands so clear, and my eagerness to comply with anything he wanted, my desire to simply please him.

For just a moment, I let myself slide my hands toward the top of my jeans. I couldn't believe just the thought of him was rousing such a reaction from me after having expelled so much from myself already. Yet, I felt full and ready again, prepared to give the man anything he asked for, to shoot any load, as many as he requested. The hardness in my jeans was again becoming unbearable, and I felt my hand moving swiftly to undo the top button—

"That's it man—turn around! Open wide," the sound of the stranger's deep voice echoed through the undecorated house from the living room, the walls reverberating with the sudden growl. Darius and the boy with the backpack may as well have been right outside my door, or next to me in bed, as the volume rose on their climax. I stopped touching myself. My cock went soft. I rolled my eyes and then closed them. If this was my reality, then I'd rather be dreaming.

In the morning, I found my way to the kitchen where Darius was standing in a jockstrap in front of the refrigerator.

"Playing soccer today?" I asked facetiously, leaning over the counter.

"Definitely got some balls on the books," Darius said, finding my eyes and smirking while he bent farther into the refrigerator to push some milk out of the way of the orange juice. He grabbed two mostly-clean glasses from the cabinet and poured us each a few ounces from the carton that undoubtedly had been sucked from by everyone in the house. "We're doing fancy breakfast today."

"What's the occasion?" I asked, searching for the cleanest part of the rim to sip from. Darius dug around for a second before he revealed a wad of cash from the front pouch of his jockstrap, presumably from somewhere tucked behind his sack. Chances were he hadn't taken a shower after last night either.

"You could have had some of this too, if you'd actually work from time to time in this work-house." He put the cash to his nose and gave it a short inhale, smiled, then tucked it away again, his most recent payment now hidden somewhere in the lockbox he had created in his underwear between his collection of money-makers.

He wasn't wrong. I wasn't certain how long it had been since I'd hooked-up with someone, for money or otherwise. If I hadn't been so frugal with the funds I had left, I would have been back on the street months ago. When I did take clients, I was always phoning it in, never present, just going through the motions of letting the other guy have a good time. But then the customers stopped booking, my unspoken language had become a pretty clear "closed for business" sign. I was tired of touching them, and they were tired of the way my body would pull back when they touched me. Long-time hook-ups dwindled to a halt and I never, ever, took walk-ins.

"It's like you hate money almost as much as you hate men." Darius kept speaking but was already done with his orange juice. He turned his attention to the wet spots near the couch and pushed at them with the toe of his sneaker, trying to discern which ones were rain water and which were something more slippery. "Not that I blame you. They do certainly make a mess."

Bundled up on the couch was one of our other roommates, Sonny, whom I rarely saw awake at all. He seemed to move from room to room like a pet, trying to find a new comfy place to settle in. In the time I'd lived here, I'd seen him go a solid eighteen hours curled in a ball. Loud music, parties, customers coming in and out—nothing seemed to bother his expert level sleep schedule. Darius grabbed a ratty sleeping bag from the floor, smelled it, and shrugged. Deeming it clean enough, he spread it over Sonny's nakedness and patted his head lovingly.

Tracing the glass circle at the top of my beverage, I knew Darius didn't expect a reply or extended conversation on the topic that had been presented. Like Sonny, I paid my portion of the rent on time for now, and that was all anyone in the house needed to know. But Darius was aware, as much as I was, that my money was running out. With the lack of jobs available in Beachside, this really was the only reasonable profession for boys like us.

"A letter came for you. Like a real letter, on paper. I didn't even know we could get mail here, but I guess they just slipped it under the door." Darius grabbed a sealed envelope from the corner of the front room. Slightly wet, like everything else in the house, the ink on the front said my full name in dripping black letters.

Careful not to destroy the contents, I used the saturation to open the envelope at the top with a single finger. Unfolding the paper inside, I saw the note was short and had an address in the center. Below that, the signature was large and filled most of the paper. It read, "Roderick."

"Who's Roderick?" Darius asked, grabbing my empty glass from me as he peaked over my shoulder. The memories flooded back quickly, but the question wasn't easy to answer. Who was Roderick? Before my life here, he was everything.

CHAPTER THREE

A s a kid, I'd often found myself collecting things. It's a reflex when you have very little to hoard the things you do, especially free things, items I could acquire from the earth. Gathering shells into an empty cup one day, I saw Roderick's shadow on the sand before I heard him speak. A summer sun beat down, and we were both standing shirtless with the waves rolling in to cover our bare feet. I'd seen him before but was always too shy to say hello, having learned to keep to myself while staying out of the house, where I'd often woke to the sound of objects being thrown against walls.

Rising, with my heap of sea treasures spilling from my styrofoam container, Roderick spoke first. "You want to make some money?" he asked.

Through the blinding sun, I nodded to his silhouette, and we were quickly picking through my collection all afternoon to find the largest pieces. We sat crossed-legged on top of a deteriorating picnic table near the beach playground, carefully selecting shells to receive a full coat of a designated color and a hastily scribbled green dollar sign.

Blue was worth the least, then purple, but it was the yellows we ended up making the most profit from. Selling them to other poor neighborhood kids, our "shell dollars" were marked up several-hundred percent, considering paint was easy enough to steal from people's sheds or the hobby store in town.

Our schemes evolved as we grew taller and could focus on adults with actual money, learning over time we shared as much of an appreciation for making quick money as we did for men. The teamwork was essential because Roderick knew how to pick them, but only I could carry it through. It was easy to rip a guy off, to pretend you were going to blow him and then run off with his wallet instead. But it became a game after a while to see how far either one of us would take a situation.

One particular evening, on the cusp of adulthood, we'd been living in the alley between a pizza place and sushi restaurant. Only one was a reasonable place for scraps, and we'd been living on garlic crust for weeks. A man invited me to his apartment, and inside it was all clear glass vases with little bubbles in them. It was countless mirrors that made the rooms look even bigger than they were. Something about the interior made me the most erect I'd ever been to that point in my life.

In most situations, I'd find the money and escape as quickly as possible. But tonight, I'd made the first move and kissed the man. I liked feeling his beard against my skin, letting him hold me in his arms in his silky sheets while Roderick waited downstairs, expecting me to run out with the goods and be ready for a quick getaway. I must have been up there for a couple hours but when I finally did make my way downstairs, Roderick was still leaning on a railing outside the swanky apartment building.

"I seriously thought you were dead up there," he said, trying to keep his tone level, but his face was full of an emotion I couldn't place. Was it anger, concern...jealousy? "Where's the money?" I held out the modest amount the man had given me in exchange for our encounter. Not only the first blowjob I'd ever given, but the first everything.

"Okay." He seemed displeased. The money in hand was an affirmation I had gone through with the original proposition that granted me entrance. "Where's the wallet though?"

The truth was, I hadn't gotten it. I'd been so overwhelmed by the experience, I hadn't even thought to grab it. I was happy to have been paid for something I actually enjoyed.

Roderick sighed and pushed himself off the railing. "So he likes them young, huh? Alright, let's hope he's rested up." He started toward the lobby entrance of the apartment building.

"You're going up there?" I asked, surprised.

"I'm not leaving without the wallet," he responded, already pushing through the door.

It was an hour later when he finally returned, wallet and payment bulging in his pocket, a satisfied smile on his face matching my own. As strong as our bond had been since meeting that day on the beach and becoming partners, something unbreakable started with the experience of losing our virginity on the same night, even if it hadn't been to each other.

There wasn't much in the letter, just the address in town not far from the alley where we used to sleep side-by-side on cold pavement together. The scrawled message simply said, "I need you." Regardless of how we left things before going our separate ways from sharing body heat in chilled alleys and undersides of bridges, I had meant it when I told him if he ever asked, I would be there.

As impressed as I was that Roderick was living in a home at all, the outside of the apartment was expectedly rough; empty bottles on the front stoop and paper bags blowing in the sea air. There were perks to living in a harbor community—edible plants and cheap ocean showers—until the natural sodium in the air began to degrade every piece of metal and make the exterior wood swell. Seagulls pecking at trash and leaving food remnants in a trail leading from the buildings to the sea, sediment and burnt oil always hanging in the air combined with the thick of something fried and salty; realistically, life there, was the worst scented candle, ever.

Six flights later, I was standing in front of a door with a crooked number barely hanging on the plaster wall. Dirt hand-prints marked the bordering walls, and vinyl flooring was peeling back around the doorframe. A dump equal to my own, but still a giant leap from the places we'd called home in the past. It seemed, alone, we were doing quite well for ourselves. Perhaps I was right when I had told him the last night we were together that I didn't need him anymore.

I was still catching my breath from the climb up the steel steps when Roderick answered my knock. He wore a wide open multi-colored housecoat and track shorts with a less than three-inch inseam. How he was balancing each ball on either side of the stitching was a mystery. But it was a look he was definitely pulling off.

"Alexander!" He instantly wrapped his arms around me, the soft fabric of his housecoat draping around my shoulders, holding us together in a furry, partially-closed cocoon for just a moment. I had forgotten how warm it felt to be against him.

From the doorway, over his shoulder, I could already see the interior of his quarters were small, but like his costume, a sort of boho-chic: tapestries on the walls, kitschy knick-knacks in every direction, and a hanging fruit basket full of ripe produce hanging in a doll-sized kitchen.

"I'm glad you got my note. I knew you wouldn't have a phone, so I didn't even bother asking around for a number," Roderick said, releasing my body to close the door and lead me to a sitting area covered in scarves and cushy floor poufs.

"Oh, and you do?" I assumed I already knew the answer as I was asking the question. He'd never had a reliable phone either. But taking in the remainder of the apartment I hadn't seen revealed a huge television on the wall, a computer, and an impressive collection of camera equipment. The lens pointed toward one of the tapestry-covered walls.

"I do now." He took out the newest possible phone from a pocket I didn't imagine his housecoat would have, the phone I'd been told people had just been waiting in line for a week before. Never the shy one, Roderick put his device down next to us on the couch and smiled. Holding my hand in his, he said, "Do you want to make some money?"

CHAPTER FOUR

"A millionaire?" I asked, looking through the lens of the camera fixed to the top of a tripod. A black image stared back at me.

"No, BILLIONAIRE," Roderick corrected, removing the cap from the front of the camera with a quick motion to reveal the framing of the tapestry and more rainbow-colored floor poufs. I hadn't noticed the array of sex toys sitting on the side tables until now, the different sizes and shapes, butt plugs and dildos. Some housed batteries and probably vibrated, others with bright jewels or tails at the end, and the thick rubber kind that wiggled when they were inside a tight hole.

He didn't spare me the details of what he'd been up to since we'd parted ways. The mysterious man tipping him the moment he entered his cam room, the gifts that started appearing at his door followed by the nightly private shows and sudden sponsorship of upgraded broadcasting equipment. The way he found new hairs on his ass by seeing it in full high-definition, and how he had learned to love each one.

"You don't know what a joy it is to pay rent and still have money left over, to not feel like you're being cheated out of your income just sending a check for your electric bill," Roderick spoke as he moved dildos around the set, cleaning them off with a spray and wipes, then stacking them on their bases in a line according to size. "Sure, he's demanding. He requires my full attention. But there's nothing like casually saying you're in the mood for pizza, having one just show up within thirty minutes, and getting paid to let him watch you enjoy it. It's full-time, but some of the easiest work I've ever done."

"So, what's the con?" I asked, not certain how much longer I was going to be able to listen to stories about his bliss knowing at some point I'd be going back home to my leaky roof and stained pillows. I stood up from my bent position where I had been looking through the camera lens to the cinematic version of Roderick. Unfiltered and back in reality, he was just as handsome as I remembered thinking he was the day we met on the beach.

He stopped arranging the silicone and polyurethane. Lifting an industrial-sized bottle of lube to slide back under the table, he said, "Well, I've been invited for something more... physical, let's say. Our mysterious billionaire friend would like me to come to his residence for the evening."

"Hopefully longer, if he's as rich as you're saying." I meant to sound optimistic, but I'm certain I sounded jealous.

"Hmm," Roderick paused for a moment, thinking something over before he spoke again. "I need you to be there tonight because I intend to grab a few things on my way out."

I had questions about why he would sabotage a good situation and steady source of income to mop a few extra bucks or wallet full of credit cards that would eventually just get cancelled. Why rip off a billionaire to take some unique dinnerware or a couple handfuls of expensive bath products, when you could keep the checks rolling in instead? But over all of that, my immediate question was, "Tonight?"

"We have a few hours to prepare, and understand, I also intend to stay on payroll after this. My concern is the sustainability of this situation. Getting too comfortable is death. Plus, he just seems a bit..." Roderick struggled for the word. It didn't seem like he was searching for the right one as much as deciding how honest he should be with me.

"A bit what?" I asked, letting myself fall ass-first onto one of the woven tweed poufs that seemed to cover at least half of the flooring in his apartment. I leaned back on my hands, spreading my knees with my feet facing toward him. I couldn't see if he was looking, but I could feel his gaze burning into my jeans, the same ones I'd been wearing the day before and were probably still stained with salty droplets.

"Intense. Yeah, let's go with intense." He cleared his throat. "Like, I don't know. He's some dude I met on the internet, and I've never seen his face. So there's that, but he's also just very particular, and I want to have a back-up plan if things get weird."

"So I'm your backup plan then?"

Instead of responding, Roderick wandered into the tiny kitchen to pull a turquoise kettle from a cabinet. "Tea?" he asked, but I knew he planned to prepare it regardless of my answer.

I nodded. He just wanted me there for security. That was it. No new con, no recreating the wheel. We were going to pull the same shit we'd been doing since we were kids, the same set-up that never seemed to get us ahead before, but—according to Roderick—was suddenly the answer to all our problems. At least I wouldn't have to get my dick out or touch anyone else's to make some money.

With two mismatched cups and saucers, Roderick joined me on one of the nearby pieces of pseudo-furniture. As comfortable as I felt, it was hard to remember we hadn't seen each other in over a year. It was even more difficult to remember the exact reason why we had stopped talking, the specific incident that had made me believe we could never be part of each other's lives again.

The tea was too hot for my mouth, but Roderick was already drinking it down, placing the cup on the saucer with a clink only to pick it right back up and continue sipping. His lips red and slightly swollen from the heat, moist and velvety from the herbs—he didn't have the kind of mouth that made it easy for men to say no.

"How dangerous is this going to be?" I asked, setting my cup on the coffee table. I wanted the truth, but I already knew I wouldn't get it.

Roderick quietly set his tea down near mine and retrieved his phone from the couch cushions where we'd been sitting before. He put it in my hand and nodded to the various forms of new technology around his place, to the endless pizza boxes he'd stacked into a shrine to his own accomplishment and formed into some sort of art installation, to the twenty-some-odd probably overpriced bohemian bean bags he'd decided to spend his money on, the nest he'd earned himself and built piece-by-piece.

"How badly do you want to get out of that rat hole you're calling a house?" he asked.

CHAPTER FIVE

I had told Roderick in the past that just because something was black didn't mean it was still indistinguishable from the darkness once it had sequins added to it. But here I was, creeping from his wrought-iron fire escape in faux-leather pants so tight they squeezed my ass cheeks and a mesh tank-top stoned with glittering rhinestones along the collar.

"It's the only black I have!" Roderick had said, throwing it at me while we were changing. There was no way that was true, but compared to the sheer catsuit he had prepared for himself, mine was definitely the more solid option. My only concern was leaving my dirty jeans at his apartment in case something went wrong and the police somehow ended up scrubbing the place for DNA evidence. Our cons had never gone that wrong, but there was always a chance they could.

From the height of the fire-escape, the sea breeze was cooling. The salty smell was almost pleasurable compared to my typical association of the ocean with poverty. Living seaside, being a beach creature, you may as well live under the ocean to anyone dwelling a few miles west. Which was exactly where we were heading in our carefully constructed attire, to the manors on the countryside where the rich people lived.

Roderick's heels clicked on the pavement in front of me, leading the way. The transparent fabric on his body allowed the breeze to flow through, pushing the hair on his chest with the direction of the wind. Even his dark beard and the peach fuzz on his ass seemed to sway with the briny air.

"Why are you wearing black, though? He knows you're coming." I was already loud-whispering, hoping my voice would carry over the light howl of the wind. We had been walking for a few miles before it occurred to me that I was the only one needing to be camouflaged during this caper.

"I look fucking cute in this," Roderick said over his shoulder. Fair enough. He did. "I have to show off my fur; it's his favorite part of me." He did a full turn in my direction as he finished speaking to run a single finger down the deep v-neck of the cat-suit through the lush forest on his chest and stomach, stopping just short of where the tight matching black briefs hugged below his belly button. I tried to remember how far the hair went down, but he turned back around before the image materialized.

Beachside was far away by the time we crossed over the train tracks. Gravel thick under our feet, I was glad I was still in my boots. At some point, we started to merge with my usual daily walk, passing the large houses and gates, the ones pushed back so only their balconies and roofs were in view from the path. I wanted to tell Roderick about my walks, about the sadness that had gotten so thick, at times I felt like I was drowning, about not being able to keep working or touch anyone, that something happened to me after we stopped relying on each other. But I said nothing, worried our codependency would return if I ever hinted at how much I needed him.

"He said to go through the woods on the side and then around the back," Roderick said, pushing himself on his hands to attempt a peek over a wall. I'd been so in my head I hadn't realized I was touching the familiar brick, that my hand had been tracing it instinctively. We had arrived at the laid stone wall with the archway and locked gate, The House of Otter.

"Are you serious? No one lives here. This place has been empty forever. Someone is playing you," I said, but Roderick was already at the end of the wall and heading into the woods. I wanted to turn around, to go back and get my jeans, take off these ridiculously tight pants, and go home. I whisper-yelled after him, "Are you in a hurry to get murdered? What if this is some sort of set-up? We don't even have flashlights!"

From the edge of the woods, Roderick pulled out his fancy phone and hit a button that created a light bright enough to guide us through the moss and roots. He smiled at me and kept walking, disappearing into the foliage.

Just being there in such close proximity to the house with the moonlight shining down made me half-hard, but also fully-terrified. And for some reason seeing Roderick take charge of the situation—telling me where to go, how, and when—was making it difficult to walk. At first, I was worried he would notice, that he would brush against me and ask me why I had a boner. But feeling him so close made me wonder what would happen if I stopped and asked him to feel it, to release me from the tightness of the pants he'd all but forced me to wear. Maybe that was the reason we were really out here.

"This house is one-hundred percent haunted. If there's anyone in there they're a ghost. They're a ghost with a ghost dick," I said, uncertain why I always felt the need to turn to humor when I was nervous.

"As long as they don't have a ghost bank account, I'm not worried," Roderick said, linking his arm in mine.

I was putting Roderick in place of the forceful man I had imagined because he was here next to me in a place I associated with being horny. It wasn't him; it was skin on my skin, something familiar mixed with my only current source of happiness. But it was also being told what to do.

"This way," he said as he continued, fearlessly leading me forward as though he had taken the route countless times. We took a sudden turn to the left and navigated a narrow dirt path only wide enough for one of us at a time. Behind him, I could see the dark curly fuzz through the fabric of his flowy catsuit, the way his round ass shifted back and forth as he pulled his heels out of the dirt with every step.

Unable to wrap himself around me, Roderick reached his hand back into mine to make sure I wouldn't lose my way as we arrived at a large courtyard. From the ray of the phone light, all I could make out at first was the large cut stones, artistry below our feet set in an array of carefully placed spirals. Then as he pointed the phone toward the structure, a covered area leading to a set of large French doors.

Following the path toward the door, Roderick flipped the phone around unexpectedly to what appeared to be a tall silhouette of a man. I jumped back, a small scream escaping my lips. Roderick's hand was over my mouth immediately.

"Calm down," he told me and walked the beam of light closer to the figure to reveal a chiseled statue of pure musculature, tufts of pebbled hair covering his body and some sort of harness around the upper portion of his frame and shoulders. Even in the dim lighting, the craftsmanship was clear; this piece was worth more than I had ever seen in my life. Whoever had once, or now did, live here—they appreciated the finer things.

Roderick handed me the phone as we got closer to the French doors, then dusted himself off from the woods. A few leaves fell out as he ran his fingers through his hair and licked his lips to make them glisten.

"What if something goes wrong and you don't have a phone?" I asked, shining the light in his direction.

"Would you rather stay out here alone in the dark?" He laughed. "Besides, who would I call?"

I shrugged. It was hard to say if Roderick had made any friends since we had stopped talking, if he had evolved in any way aside from financially since the period of time when we were all the other had in the world. He owned enough seating in his house for a tea party, that was for sure. But possibly he had no one to share it with, no one to offer weird tea and a rainbow floor cushion.

"If I'm not back in two hours, find me," he said. I looked down at the time on the phone: 12 a.m.

"Don't you want to wait like five minutes? You cannot enter a spooky poorly-lit house at exactly midnight. There are rules for these things. Some hookup handbook about not letting a friend be involved with your homicide?" My whisper-shouting ineffective, Roderick put a finger to his lips, telling me to be quiet.

"Funny. Normally this would be the other way around." He smiled and turned the knob. White flowing drapes flapped from the interior of the door in the autumn breeze, circling around him for just a moment until the door was closed, and he was gone.

With the drapes settled, I thought about what he said. This was the first time I found myself playing bodyguard for him. I couldn't imagine what Roderick had done all those times I'd gone upstairs and taken hours longer than I should have. But with him inside, I settled into the darkness alone with my new best friend—the super hot stone guy in the courtyard.

CHAPTER SIX

Living in luxury meant feeling dew form on the grass, without the humidity of living near sand. It meant being able to build a house made of heavy material minus the fear of it sinking too far below sea-level and being swallowed by a sinkhole. It was lush greenery and trees with thick trunks; leaves that didn't feel like they had been spawned from bay water. But most importantly, flowers, real flowers—not just weeds that budded. Out in the courtyard, all around me, there were curated colorful blossoms.

Aside from the perennials, one of the best things I discovered while exploring the grounds outside with the phone flashlight was there were virtually no bugs at all, no mosquitos or horse-flies, even though we were only miles from the shore. Which was good because over an hour had passed since Roderick had entered the house, and if we had been at home, I would have been devoured by now.

So far, I hadn't seen any lights from the windows or heard any sounds escape. Everything still seemed dark and uninhab-ited. I wondered for a while if there was a chance Roderick had gotten lost inside without the light, that perhaps he was stuck just inside the back entrance, feeling around for the doorknob to find his way back to the courtyard. There was still a strong possibility that this whole thing had been some sort of set-up. I hadn't thought to ask Roderick before agreeing to this if he had made any enemies recently. What if they had gotten him inside this abandoned house and were hurting him? He could be lying in the middle of the floor waiting for me to rescue him while I was out here admiring topiaries.

The darkness allowed my mind to fill with anxiety and panic. Circling past the stone man as I paced around, revealed more silhouettes in the distance. I discovered another man in a harness, but smaller, less muscle-bound, and on his knees. Furry but thin, the statue had something in his mouth, some sort of rounded ball attached to a strap that fastened around the back of his head. His hands were tied behind him. The artist had taken great detail in the expression of his eyes, a mix of surprise, excitement, and fear.

It was nearly 2 a.m. and the phone battery was drained from having the light on the entire time. At this rate, we'd have nothing left for the walk back through the woods and to the apartment. I hadn't thought of using the phone as anything aside from a light and truthfully didn't really know how it worked even if I did want to snoop. The cell phones I'd used, when I'd found the money to afford them, had been the type that only received calls and the variety of texts that had to be typed-out using the number pad. Luckily, Roderick had left the flashlight controls up for me. I found a spot near the door, leaned against the smooth stone of the exterior wall, and in an attempt to conserve our resources clicked the "OFF" button on my only reprieve from the darkness.

My other senses heightened from the lack of sight, I could smell the flowers in the night air, the wet dirt and thick grass. I could hear the chirps of crickets and croak of something in the distance. I'd never found water in the woods during my walks, but I had also never been this far out. It hadn't crossed my mind to venture this deep, to see if there was a way into the house. Before now, the structure had stood as impenetrable and only to be admired from a distance. Being this close, sitting just outside what only yesterday was the source of my arousal, I could feel myself tightening in the black pants again.

Growing thicker, I laughed at myself. The two hour mark was close, and I needed to develop a rescue plan, not jerk-off outside some old house like I had a fetish for architecture. It was then my sense of touch was activated. Something brushed against my leg, gliding over the faux-leather pants. I shifted my weight and scooted a few inches away from the sensation, assuming it was a gust of wind or a fallen tree branch with leaves pointing toward me, something I hadn't seen before I sat. But the sensation returned, and this time, it was directly on my half-hard cock, rubbing lightly over the zipper and tugging at the button above it.

I jumped quickly, but my body was blocked against something firm and directly in front of me. It pushed on my shoulder, landing me back against the wall. A voice said, with force, "Sit down boy," and continued to unbutton my pants. I could feel his breath close to me as he spoke. Fumbling for the phone, I struggled for light as he kept his firm hold on me.

The phone leapt from my hands and directly to the stone ground with a terrible crash that made us both jolt. In that quick moment, I rolled to the side and out from under him. Feeling around for the phone but finding the door knob instead, I turned it quickly and let myself fall inside. The white drapes fluttered as I jumped up quickly to close the door behind me. Unsure whether the person would follow, I looked quickly around the interior for an escape. One red light was in the distance, and I ran straight for it, my boots heavy against what felt like slippery tile.

With little illumination, I kept my pace down a hallway that seemed to stretch on forever, putting the red light farther and farther from my reach. There seemed to be no other light inside, so this had to be where Roderick was. I yelled for him through my panting with no response. My own voice echoed back at me against the flooring. As I yelled for him, I tripped and fell through the doorframe of the room I had been attempting to reach. From behind me, heavy footsteps approached, then stopped. I struggled from the floor, attempting to get to my feet, but his hands were already around my ankles. My face and hands slid across the tile as he dragged me.

His strength surpassed my own, which made an easy task of pulling off the mesh tank-top I had been wearing to blend in with the night and wrapping it around my wrists. In the red light, I could see a giant X bathed in crimson and adorned with straps on each end. He lifted and heaved me to the structure, parting my legs and fastening them to either side. From behind, he removed the tank-top rope only to grab each one of my hands to complete the X and put them in their own buckles, velvety but tight around my wrists with what felt like a metal clasp joining the material.

Coming out of what must have been shock, I began screaming again for Roderick, for help, the total nonsense people yell when they are terrified. With my mouth wide-open in mid plea of, "Who are you? What are you doing? Let me go!" I felt the mesh tank-top go straight inside, forcing my tongue flat in my mouth so I couldn't push the fabric out. I was muted and completely immobile.

Without me struggling, he took his time undoing the metal button of the pants I had borrowed from Roderick. He circled his finger around the hair just above the band, slipping one finger through where a belt would normally be just to feel the tightness. Then he let both his hands slide around to grab at each of my ass cheeks and give them a squeeze. The zipper came down last, and as he brushed the hair around my cock, I was hard again.

My saliva soaking the mesh shirt, I didn't want to moan when he started stroking me, but I knew he could hear me through the mesh. The pre-cum leaking out creating a smoothness between his fingertip and my foreskin, I should have been trying more desperately to get loose. But my cock disagreed, and as he continued teasing and pumping with the liquid dripping out of me, I was getting firmer.

I couldn't see his face, but the voice was the same. It was his words that made it impossible not to finally release. Slowly, with a tight fist around me, he said, "Do it, boy. Give me that load. Now."

My entire body shuddered as I came, my hands balled into fists and toes arched off the safety of the small platforms I had been braced on below the straps. Everything went black.

CHAPTER SEVEN

It was my hearing that came back first, the sound of Roderick's voice saying, "Are you okay?"

The man had just left me there, suspended and tied down. At least Roderick found me in the house. Maybe there was still a chance we could get out if the man had released him, or better, never found him at all.

"Where's the phone?" he asked. "It's so dark."

The next of my senses to return was touch, and more specifically, one side of the French door smacking against the back of my head as Roderick forced it further open to scramble around on the ground searching for a source of light. I was back outside, but had no memory of how I had gotten there.

He was fumbling with the phone against the stone, and after a few seconds, the beam was being cast over my closed eyes. I opened them slowly. Roderick was above me, looking exactly the same as when he had entered the house.

"Stellar bodyguard you are. Did you seriously fall asleep out here?" he asked. I didn't even know how to answer the question.

"What time is it?" I managed to get out instead. Roderick looked at the clock on the phone.

"I could've been dead in there. It's twenty after two." He sounded reasonably agitated. "Not that it matters. He didn't even touch me. But I got the money." He lowered a stack of bills in my direction on the ground and shook them like a fan. I was still blinking my eyes, unsure of how it could possibly be just after two in the morning when my time with the man had felt endless.

"Let's go before this battery runs out," he said, reaching out his hand for mine. I wanted to tell him everything, about the man and the giant X, being dragged across the floor by my ankles, and more importantly, completely ruining the crotch region of his favorite black pants by cumming all over them. But back in the courtyard with the stone statues and flowers, the hum of late night turning into early morning, it all seemed less real now.

With Roderick there and unaffected, my shirt was still in place; nothing seemed different from right before the moment I had felt the man's presence near me in front of the door. Aside from the sense of relief in my body, the relaxation that usually came paired with an extended walk in the woods, it was pretty apparent I had never actually been in the house at all.

We were halfway through the woods before I was awake enough to start asking questions, but Roderick began filling me in from the second we were out of earshot of the house. He told me about the kind of information you can get out of a man depending on what you show him you can fit in your mouth. About the replicated array of toys matching the set-up in his own house, that had been displayed in perfect order and prepared for him to use. And that the room he was directed to stay in was almost identical to the start of the dream apartment he had constructed. He told me that, all-in-all, it had felt like being in a cam session, just with the man in the actual room to instruct him.

"I still have no idea what he looks like, but he honestly sounds kind of hot." He nearly tripped over a root as he spoke.

Side-shuffling into some ground-cover, it wrapped around his heel before he shook it off, and we found our way back to the main path.

"The money was just laying there ready on a dresser before I even started taking off my clothes." He didn't have pockets but had shoved stacks of bills into the piece of long black ribbon he'd turned into a makeshift belt to create a waistline.

"He knows the money gets me hard, so he told me the entire dresser was full of cash. It definitely worked." He sounded like he was smiling. I was still reeling from rejoining reality after how vivid my dream felt, but this world was starting to get just as strange. I had figured, knowing Roderick, he was going to grab some stupid tablecloth or jewelry to sell. I hadn't imagined he'd be bold enough to grab the guy's wallet like we had pulled in the past. Or to actually mop real money from the guy he'd self-described as "intense."

"Okay, so I may have taken a little more than he told me to," he admitted. This was a one-sided conversation. "But he told me the money was all going to be mine eventually anyway."

"Alright, okay." He was reacting to my silence. "I took a lot more than he told me to, but it's not the same as stealing if it was already mine!" He wasn't trying to convince me. "You know, just because you're not talking doesn't mean you're not coming off as bitchy."

We didn't speak again until we reached the edge of the woods and the brick wall was in view. This time, I didn't run my hand along it as we walked. I didn't look toward the arches of the top of the house to admire them. We were edging closer to the main road when the phone died and the light went out, around the same time I decided I would have to find a new place to take my walks after tonight.

"Well, that's fucking great." I had obviously struck a nerve in Roderick. Tension was high, but I knew we needed to talk through the darkness, use the sound of each other's voices like sonar to figure out where we were going.

"What if he figures out how much you took? Aren't you worried at all that this guy knows where you live?" I finally asked the question I should have asked before we left Roderick's apartment to pull off this ill-conceived heist.

"He's never been there." He said this with such nonchalance as we encroached closer to the railroad tracks that it made me stop where I stood. I kept in place until he turned around, alerted by the suddenness of the sound of my footsteps no longer following behind him.

"If he's sent you a pizza, he knows your address." Even in the moonlight, I couldn't see his reaction but his stillness matching mine made it apparent. Now he was worried too.

Our pace continued forward, the sea breeze getting thicker and the sounds of the ocean becoming more distinct. The toe of my boot stubbed against something solid, and in the same moment, Roderick screamed and fell to the pebble near me. We'd found the train tracks.

"I tripped," he said matter-of-factly, with a slight whine. He'd honestly had quite a night already, and I knew I was being tough on him. Shuffling my way toward the sound of his voice, I helped him up, and together we navigated the blackness of the night over the metal railings, my arm wrapped around his back and his around my shoulder, our bodies pressed together at the side, the friction of our outfits creating warmth between us in the night air.

The streetlights became more luminous as we approached the outskirts of town. In the distance, the moon still hung high, but the sun seemed to be considering rising over the sea, tempted to begin its journey to create a new day. Bathed in faded hues of orange and blue light, we climbed the fire escape back to the backdoor of his apartment. Changing out of our caper costumes, I grabbed up my jeans and forced a leg inside.

Roderick stood next to me, the other pant leg around my ankle and shirt barely over my head. "Can you stay the night?" he asked.

"You mean the morning?" I wasn't sure if I was trying to be funny, but I knew he was being sincere with his question, that he was actually afraid the man may notice the missing money and come after him.

"Just in case?" He hadn't finished dressing either, and while I should have been looking at his eyes, instead I was focused on his chest and nipples. My focus pulled to the moist hair covering him and how it rose and fell with his breath, the sweaty fur as dark and thick as the beard and mustache framing his lips.

His heart seemed to be beating quickly, either from the fear he had brought upon himself or the fact that he had forced us both on our exit and entrance to use the fire escape instead of the front door in the off-chance someone in his building was questioned about whether or not he had left that night. As if the cops would make it a priority to ask them if he'd had the opportunity to rob the eccentric billionaire down the road that no one actually believed existed.

I had already decided that after tonight, I would never tell a soul there was someone actually living in that house. Even though I couldn't convince Roderick, something in me knew the billionaire he'd connected with was not the type to get involved with the law. If I were in Roderick's position, it wouldn't have been the police I was worried about finding me anyway.

I wanted him to be safe, to know for sure that the next time we saw each other wouldn't be at his memorial service. But to stay to keep watch over him would mean falling back into old habits and a full day of trying to avoid looking at his body with the sun shining. I wasn't sure when I would see him again, but I knew if I stayed, I would never want to leave.

"I can't," I said, forcing myself to break my gaze and look at his face. "I just... can't." With my share of the money shoved in my pocket, I finished putting on my pants and allowed the varying shades of dawn to guide me home.

CHAPTER EIGHT

Three in the afternoon often felt like breakfast time, not just for me, but for the entire house. Not that breakfast was more than a shared pot of black coffee and a few cigarettes for most of the boys, all bent over the high-top counter and gossiping about the men they had seen the night before, elbows on formica and dirty coffee mugs. There were rarely names during the conversation, just dollar amounts and endless dishing about how a quick handjob became Mr. Fries and a Shake; or how something more intimate or lengthy was Mr. Internet Bill; or for the rare overnight stay, a man could even become Mr. This Month's Rent, especially if he was into fetishy stuff he could never ask his husband, or wife, to do to him.

"I'll ride any face for a new comforter and set of pillows at this point," Darius said, spinning a spoon around his coffee, as if we had milk or sugar in the house to mix into the liquid. He pulled it up and licked the metal clean, letting it slide down his tongue. It was a reflex of the job, always being sexy, always being on. "They're getting empty and flat, and I know it's about to get cold again."

"Beachside winters are not even winters though. You don't need a blanket. You need a hammock and some coconuts," Brent said, swishing around what was left of the carton of orange juice

Darius and I had killed the day before. He looked directly at me in a way that said, *I know you drank this*, but didn't say it out loud. Instead, he took the last swig, crushed the cardboard in his fist, and threw it in the trash.

Marco watched him and added, "Then Alexander can move outside to the hammock since we know he's about to miss his rent."

Why the brothers had decided to move this far south after growing up in a place north enough to have real seasons, I had never understood. But Brent and Marco seemed to love it here. Despite being so broke they shared a room and twin mattress on the floor, they maintained the tanning was better and so were the men. They had this idea that *season*, meaning the time period where it's cold everywhere else so people come to Beachside for vacation, was going to be peak money.

There was a knock at the door, and immediately Marco popped up. "The bleach is here," he said, running through the front room.

"Am I the only one that isn't getting mail here?" Darius said, throwing up his hands. "I thought they said it was too *dangerous* out here for that." I shrugged in acknowledgement. He said dangerous like he was mocking the type of people that were afraid to be out this way. Beachside was considered the bad area of the county we shared with all the rich folk and their mansions, but we were living in the worse side of the bad part of town.

Marco turned back from the door, looking at Brent, "How much did you order? We only need to dye it once." We all walked to the door to see the front stoop full of cardboard boxes. None of them had labels, but unless those idiots had accidentally ordered a few palettes-worth, it definitely wasn't hair dye. There didn't seem to be a delivery truck or person nearby, just a folded paper on the closest box. Brent reached down and unfolded it.

"They're for you," he said, looking at me. This was the first time I had ever seen him read. Before that moment, I wasn't certain he could.

"Whoa, who you been fucking?" Marco said, poking me in the ribs with his brawny elbow. He always smelled like lemon juice, the kind with preservatives added. Darius was still the only one who knew the answer to Marco's question was: *no one.*

None of us had changed into real clothes. We'd been brunching in underwear and jockstraps, and most days that was the nearest any of us got to an outfit inside the house. But with no hesitation, everyone was out on the porch helping me load the boxes inside, giving the neighbors an unobstructed view of whatever we had worn to bed the night before. Even Sonny, who had been curled into a blanket full of holes on the dirty couch, got up and wrapped the blanket around his waist like a long towel. He let it fall off his hips as he lifted something heavy to his chest and continued dick-and-ass-out all the way into the house. His contribution being complete, Sonny gave us all a tired smile and snuggled back up into his cozy spot.

"Like having a cat that pays bills," Darius said, running his fingers through Sonny's long brown hair. He was already lightly snoring.

"The note said to open the biggest one first," Brent said, like he was the leader in the escape room that had become my mysterious delivery.

"Did it say who it was from at all?" I asked. He shook his head while Marco identified and pointed at the biggest box.

Slicing open the packing tape, another folded note appeared at the top of layers of foam packing peanuts. The message was hand-written and said,

> *Follow these instructions exactly.*
> *Assemble everything and turn it on.*

I'm waiting.

I couldn't remember the last time I had received a gift, and the anonymity of the sender made the entire thing even stranger. Digging further into the box, I found cables and a little further down, what seemed to be a small camera. Marco opened a long, thin box, "It's a tripod," he said, pulling it out with a storm of packing peanuts. "And I think that's a webcam," he said, motioning toward what I had unboxed.

They were passing around an old steak knife now, taking turns opening the boxes closest to them. "Dude, there's a whole computer in here." Brent had gotten one of the larger boxes.

"Oh girl, this camera is brand-new!" Darius was already attaching the strap and putting it around his neck.

Technology was never among my talents, but eventually with the help of the boys we were able to connect everything to the specifications and instructions we found in the boxes with the equipment. Luckily, we were still able to steal a signal from the house next door to get online. With all the right lights blinking, we powered on the computer. A window with a single video file opened first, titled, "Watch Alone."

"Wow, okay." Darius was personally offended after having spent the entire afternoon helping me connect all the right cords and boxes together.

"But for real, you have no idea who this sugar daddy is who sent you all this stuff?" Marco asked. I had told them over and over I didn't know where it came from. I didn't have a sugar daddy. I'd never had a sugar daddy. But I shook my head again to answer the question.

"Well let me know if Daddy is looking for some more underprivileged youth to sponsor, because damn," Brent said, his hands on his hips, taking in everything we'd put together. "I guess this means you won't need that hammock."

Darius seemed more concerned than the other boys, and while he shuffled the others out to leave me to it, he said, "Is there a chance this could be from your parents? A peace offering?"

I wanted the answer to his question to be yes, to think there was a shot my family was trying to reconnect, that someone had hit the Beachside Lottery and decided to use the opportunity to reach out to me via pricey gifts. But I knew the chances of that were slim after so many years.

Darius shut the door behind him as I played the video file and heard the recorded voice instructing me on my next steps. I didn't know how it was possible, but I suddenly knew exactly who had sent the gifts.

CHAPTER NINE

"Hello?" I had opened the software and followed the directions the voice had given me but still, the screen was black.

"Good job, boy." A familiar voice was live and coming out of the speakers.

"Who is this?" I asked, as if I hadn't heard the same voice the night before while I was waiting for Roderick to finish inside the house. The voice didn't respond. "How did you know where I live?"

A short inhale from the speakers, "You're asking a lot of questions when you should be saying thank you."

I stopped talking. The math had already been done by the boys during the set-up on exactly how much I could make off this stuff. Resale, pawn-shop, store credit return: I had options after this interaction. My privacy had been violated, and I wanted answers.

"You're a very private boy, aren't you?" It seemed like he was going to keep talking. The black screen on the window didn't change, but I could hear him moving around. Sounds like metal clinking together, rubber or straps sliding, like the noises I heard when I dreamt I attached to the cross, the giant wooden

X. "Perhaps you prefer: independent?" he said with a jingle of some hardware followed by a laugh.

"What do you want me to do with all this stuff?" I asked, ignoring his question.

"It's yours to do with as you wish. It's a line of communication for us, no strings attached after this conversation. Everything, like the money you stole from me the other night, is yours to keep."

"I didn't take your money."

"Don't misunderstand, boy. I'm not upset. I expected your friend to take more than was instructed. I'm just glad he had the sense to share it with you. I wasn't certain I could trust him to do that."

"Is this what you did when you met him? Sent him all this stuff to get his attention?"

"Do I have yours?"

I shifted on the bed, forgetting that even though I couldn't see him, he could still see me. It hadn't crossed my mind to change out of my underwear or to put on a shirt before opening the video. I hadn't realized the webcam was going to turn on.

I'd been acting annoyed with his gifts. As if he were inconveniencing me. But from the second he began speaking, my mind wandered to what my imagination had created, our time together in the house and the seemingly now real myth of the owner of the mansion I'd made into the object of so much affection. Before I'd learned he actually existed, I wanted so badly to know what he desired, to understand what he did inside that house and who, if anyone, kept him company.

Even if our session had never actually happened, I'd gotten the voice right. The deep rich sound of his tone from across the internet connection may as well have been whispering in my ear in that dark red-lit room. I shifted again, trying to hide the firmness building under the flimsy white briefs I'd been wearing since yesterday.

"Take out your cock, boy."

Even as I was doing it, I didn't understand why I was listening to him, what turned me on about him demanding things from me, buying my time and attention. But I wanted to obey. I wanted to know my body and time were worth more than I had ever gotten handed to me for a quick pound on a dirty mattress. I was harder now, leaning my head on my hand. My weight was balanced on my side, facing the camera as I let my cock slide out of the top of the elastic keeping it against my abdomen, almost making it look like an accident as I stared directly into the camera lens above the computer screen.

"Very nice, boy," he said from the other side of the black window. I could hear more shuffling around and from just his inflection, I could tell he was smiling. Licking a broad stroke across my palm, I rubbed the saliva over my head and a little of the shaft. My finger slid up my stomach to my nipples and circled each one, letting my hand grasp more firmly against the pulsing sensation that was building.

"Stroke, now," he directed. I obeyed and began rubbing furiously. My own spit and dripping pre-cum mixed into a perfect lubricant. It was rare for me to reach this point so quickly, but knowing he was watching, that he was demanding this show, I already wanted to cum. Just not until he asked me to.

"You're going to hold it until I want it," he said as if he could read my mind. "You're going to shoot even harder than the last time."

I wasn't sure what last time he was talking about, but I didn't have blood left in my brain to process the possibilities. Every ounce of my blood seemed to be in my cock, making me rock hard. Still stroking furiously, pinching my nipples harder and feeling my balls so full they were ready to explode, I needed his permission.

"Now, boy. Give me that load. It's mine. It belongs to me. Do it."

The release was instantaneous to his command, and I shot hard all over my chest. Droplets reached my neck and chin. I wasn't certain how good the resolution was on his end, if he could see the cum all over my body and face.

"Show me how good you taste, boy," the black screen demanded. I scooped a smaller dot from my chin and pushed into my mouth. Sucking it hard and swallowing the salty but sweet flavor of myself, I imagined he was forcing it on my tongue, this man I had never seen but was already so real in my head.

Still covered in my own cum he said, "You're coming back tomorrow."

I was out of breath when I asked him, "What about Roderick?"

"He can't be trusted."

It wasn't my first instinct to take Roderick's job, but it sounded like he had lost it on his own. I thought about Roderick's apartment and everything in it. The new outfits and tea kettle and stupid little tweed poufs all over the hardwood floor. I thought about the things I deserved in exchange for my time. If Roderick was going to lose the income whether I took the job or not, maybe it was my turn to have something good happen.

As I considered the proposition, there was a quick knock on my door. Before I could say to enter, Darius was there clicking a glass of orange juice against his nails and whispering, "Dinner?" like a real question. Someone must have run out for more while I was interacting with the man. It felt like only a few minutes, but I could see through my window that night had fallen.

Noticing me lying there covered in my own cum, Darius covered his mouth and in full-volume said, "Oh, oh, okay," then shut the door behind him. He didn't know he was in view of the camera standing in the doorway. I was immediately worried I had violated some sort of protocol or instruction, that my opportunity was over before it had begun. A few seconds of agonizing silence followed.

"You're such a good boy," the voice finally said. "I could never spoil a boy like that one, decent beard potential, but not enough fur. The boys you're living with right now. They'll give it to anyone with a ten dollar bill. You're not like them; you're special."

There was a short silence again, but during this one, I smiled. I made sure he could see how happy he had already made me. "Tomorrow," he said. "You know where to go."

Then the black box was gone.

CHAPTER TEN

S omething that had been proven the other night: it was easier to navigate the walk during the day. The man hadn't specified a time, so I left the house as if I was just going for my typical stroll. The duration of the journey allowed me to drift in and out of excitement crossfaded with concern. I had already decided that going forward with the man's requests was not a direct betrayal to Roderick. It was uncertain to me why I hadn't been put through the same trial, why the man had invited me to meet him in person directly after our first interaction. He had said he saw something in me. Perhaps he didn't feel the need to test me any further. Yet, I worried how much my former partner-in-crime had told him, if I'd ever come up during their cam sessions. There was still a chance the man knew; if this had been just a couple years ago, Roderick and I would have worked as a team to take him for every cent.

In the daylight, the house appeared less sinister than it had in the darkness. Much less *abandoned Victorian estate with a horrifying backstory* and more *potentially hot rich guy that enjoys his privacy*. The wall leading to the wooded area seemed once again inviting enough for me to reach out and run my fingers across, if only for a moment. In the safety of the canopy, I could pick out the different trees I had used to lean my back against so many times, before I knew the wonders that lived only a few hundred more feet into the depth. The journey to the courtyard was lined with crusted spots in the dirt that still wore the mark of my visits. The indent of my boots were still prints in the soil, spread in a wide-stance to frame the splatter pattern.

Curving around to the left, the path to the back of the house wasn't as easy to find as Roderick had made it seem. Somehow despite not having a map or clear lighting, he had instinctively known the way. Eventually I located the small dirt path, just wide enough for a single person, with tall hedges on either side. Sun barely shined through the denseness of the forest onto the loose sentiment below as I let my hands grab onto the tight brush surrounding me. The labyrinth wound in a disorienting zig-zag until it eventually spit me out into a clearing full of stone men. I hadn't seen all of them last night, the dozens that stood, kneeled, or lay in the grassy open garden. The flowers surrounded each one like a shrine and all had harnesses or straps, leather and latex depicted in earthen detail, beards and scruff expertly chiseled into the polished rock.

Part of me wanted to stay and admire them, give my attention to their individual uniqueness, but behind me, the back French doors were already open. The sheer white curtains, blowing in the wind. From inside, music; something classical, violins and wooden instruments, beckoning me to enter. I didn't want to keep him waiting.

Following the music, I crossed the threshold I'd fallen asleep on the evening before, still unsure if I had dreamed or actually been part of the encounter in the red room. Inside, I looked to my right toward the long hallway I had run through, the one that seemed to stretch endlessly as I ran for the light. To my surprise, in place of the hallway from my dream, there was a wall. No hallway, no door, and yet the same tile flooring I could still feel a burn on my cheek from being dragged across, but meeting at a sharp corner with the tile, just a flat wall with a long table pushed against it. I was sure now: I had absolutely imagined the entire thing.

Walking toward the table; it was full of fresh magenta and gold flowers with long thick stems. Well-hydrated and obviously looked after with care, they were displayed in tall transparent vases on either side. Between them on the table lay a beautifully hand-written note in the center that read,

> *Your room is on the top floor of the east wing.*
> *Make yourself comfortable.*

The marble stairs began wide and welcoming at the ground level and split after about thirty steps. Taking the fork right and climbing to the second floor of the house, I tried every door until one finally opened. Everything else had been locked, and even when I knocked, there was no reply. As strange as it seemed to be in the house at all, it was more odd to be completely alone, to hear my own knock and voice accompanied by nothing more than the constant soundtrack in every hallway and staircase. He hadn't been there to welcome me when I arrived, but this orchestrated scavenger hunt through his home made me wonder if he would eventually be the prize.

My first observation of the only unlocked room was saturation of color inside, the array of hues that flooded the variety of cushiony spaces: a four-poster king-sized bed with a canopy in bright blue, a sitting area with couches and chairs in maroon, a bathroom with a walk-in shower with detailed gold tiles, and a purple claw-foot tub. The bathroom was bigger than any house I had lived in at any point in my life.

Another hand-written note on the bed said,

> *You can have anything you wish.*

Pick up the phone and simply ask.

The phone was cream and corded. An earpiece and receiver with gold accents completed the vintage style, not because it was old, but because it was classy as fuck, like everything else in this house. Vibrant and colorful. Elegance sitting somewhere just before tacky. Balance mixed with extravagance.

I didn't know when he would arrive, but my first instinct was to get in the bathtub, to be clean and ready for him. The basin was deep and took a few minutes to fill. Pulling with my big toe at the gold chain leading to the drain plug, I knew what I was missing. I hopped out, wet and naked, to pick-up the vintage phone.

"Hello?" I said with some hesitation. No one replied, but I could hear breathing. "Um... could I please have some bubbles?"

Immediately, there was a knock on the door as if my request had been anticipated. I opened it up to find a glass container of something tinted light purple sitting on a silver tray, corked and curved, with a single loop handle, like a genie bottle from cartoons I'd seen as a kid. But I didn't see anyone. "Thank you!" I yelled down either side of the abandoned hallway. My own voice echoed back with the violins supporting it.

Thick suds came fast under the running water and smelled like the blossoms outside in the courtyard. Lavender, peony, something fuschia or plum, small and delicate. As if they'd been crushed between stones for hours to create the subtle aroma of the soap, but paired with something more, something rough and masculine, like sawdust and chopped wood. I let the expertly-crafted musk engulf my senses while the hot water and foam swallowed me inside. Sighing a long deep exhale, I realized I'd been smiling since the moment I walked into the house.

After my bath, I'd figured I would towel off and put on the same jeans and shirt I'd been wearing for days, but picking up the heap of them now, they were malodorous and offensive compared to the fragrance sticking to my skin and body hair.

Naked for a while, I opened a large wooden wardrobe across from the bed to find a lovely black robe, soft and soothing, like a blanket with arm holes. Opposite the hanging robe, shirts hung organized by color, collared and casual, in all shades. Below them in drawers lay the fit of jeans I liked, the kind that grabbed my ass in the right places. All brand new.

Other drawers were full of backless underwear, all in my size, some cloth, some made of neoprene or shining plastic. Trying on a collection of them, I worried I was invading someone's curated apparel, that perhaps all of this was not intended for me to have a fashion show. I was, after all, a guest in this house. But seeing my reflection in the oblong mirror standing in the corner, the way my ass was framed in every jockstrap perfectly, I knew he had picked out everything just for me, like he knew my taste better than I knew my own. He had bought me everything I would have picked out for myself if I'd had the money to spend.

Positioned off to the side of the large bed, a television so big I questioned its stability was mounted to the exposed brick. Using the variety of controls in the bedside table, I picked a movie and settled into my robe—my body scented like a husky lumberjack with a flower tucked behind his ear. I waited for the man to come, to smell me, to take my holes in this huge bed. So much of me wanted to try, to allow someone inside after so long. But he never came.

My hair was already dry, and my stomach was empty. I hadn't stayed long enough into the afternoon to take in the usual coffee breakfast with my housemates. It had been at least two days since I'd consumed much at all. Now I was here, and I was going to take advantage of the amenities.

I picked up the cream and gold phone again, "Could I have a sandwich please?" Breathing on the other end of the phone then a click. After a few minutes, another knock on the door and on a silver tray, the most gigantic sandwich I'd ever seen. Layers of fresh soft bread and sauces, delicately cut vegetables paired with warm tea in a detailed cup with a floral pattern and matching cream pitcher. Taking it inside, I wondered if this was the type of treatment Roderick had been only days from accepting as his own, that perhaps this had all been prepared for him initially, and the fact that he'd stolen the money had allowed me to take his place. He had put in the time, but I was living his reward.

Despite the opulence of my surroundings, Roderick seemed to find his way into my thoughts. I wasn't sure what I would say to him the next time we met, if we ever did meet again. Perhaps I had something I needed to apologize for, taking this right out from under him. But the items in the room were obviously curated for me, not him, and I allowed this thought to soothe me as the warm tea coated my insides. I convinced myself I was as special as the decor and clothing was letting me believe until my sandwich was just crumbs on the silver tray, and I fell asleep.

CHAPTER ELEVEN

D ays passed in what seemed like an endless cycle of movies, delicious food, and glorious bubble baths. As far as I knew, no rules were in place to keep me inside the room, but I still didn't want to push any boundaries. After mornings of soft biscuits with preserves and nights with chocolate cherries, I figured it would be nice to at least thank the people preparing my meals, so I used that as my excuse for the occasional walks I took around the mansion. My exploration revealed no workers or servants—no other people at all. No one was visibly maintaining the house or courtyard. As I had observed while I was surveying the house from afar, not a soul seemed to come or go, but they had to be living here, somewhere.

The majority of doors remained sealed, aside from my own and some entrances to larger portions of the house. Every wing unveiled more hallways leading to the occasional open library full of paintings or sculptures. I was learning about the man before even meeting him by wandering his chosen antiquities, his collected art and unique pieces, the items he decided to surround himself with in this household. It occurred to me at some point, with no new handwritten notes appearing, that the man was probably rarely there at all. To have billions of dollars meant to never have to call one place home. It meant having the means to create a space like this in every part of the world.

I felt a longing to hear his voice again and craved his attention, to let him know how much I appreciated the gifts and to apologize for my attitude when we had spoken over the camera. His home had made me understand his deep need for happiness, and my sudden urgency to fill that space. I found myself suddenly in lust with the idea of an endlessly wealthy man seeking fulfillment, his collection telling me that sex was a hole in his life he longed to satisfy. I made it my mission to find clues, to learn his questions and become his answer.

The library provided information, the sort of literature a lonely man would collect for himself. Further inspection of the cabinet in my room filled with harnesses, collars, and leashes provided more. I would become this object of affection, his favorite toy. It would be my quest to earn everything he had already given to me and more.

I was in a deep sleep when I was awoken by a knock on the door. Outside, on another silver tray, lay a folded note,

> *Mr. Usher requests the blue harness*
> *and your presence in this location.*

Below the words was a hand drawn map of a section of the house and a marked path leading to a room with a huge red X over it.

The man had never told me his name, and I hadn't asked. There had been nothing penned with his first nor last name around the expansive house. If he had family or the type of surname that should be well-known, it had been kept from this place intentionally. This altar to his more personal life held no indications of who he could be anywhere else. Perhaps that's where he had been all this time while I was here alone, some-where handling whatever business afforded him this luxury.

He hadn't specified, but I wondered if that's what I should call him when we finally did meet in person. *Mr. Usher. Mr. Usher, Sir? Mr. Usher, Keeper of Bubbles and Fancy Sandwiches.* The winning golden ticket I found on the floor of my former best friend's life. It was difficult to understand how this mys-terious man had become my entire world so quickly when I hadn't even been given his name before this moment. I won-dered if Roderick knew it, if he had gotten that far. So much of me wanted to know if his experience had been at all similar to mine before Usher decided to cut him off.

The color-coding made it easy to find the requested gear: a harness with two loops on the back and a ring in the center on both sides, and a jockstrap to match with a zipper on the front for easy access. I wanted to at least appear modest while I walked through the house, not bore him with my nudity. In honesty, as much of me wanted to offer him payment for every-thing I had been given, there was so much more of me that was still worried about being touched. The months that had passed since a man had put his hands on me, since a hand that wasn't my own had allowed me to climax—I wasn't certain I could do it again. But I wanted to. I wanted to try—for him.

There was a satin robe matching the fluffier one in the closet, black with a ribbon to tie around my waist. It covered my ass just below the cheeks, leaving my upper-chest exposed. I intended to be a dish he had to uncover, for him to picture me as one of the silver trays my food and gifts appeared on with a matching cover ready to be lifted at any pace he desired.

I walked the house in the darkness. The typical piano or violin music was absent and only low ominous tones replaced it. Everything on the first floor was bathed in the familiar red-light, the one I was certain I had created with my imagination.

The tones too seemed unreal after hearing the relaxing classical instrumentations throughout the days and nights. They made me nervous and full of anxiety, as if the sense of leisure I'd achieved had never happened at all.

It seemed odd though, that even in this sudden haunted vibe of the house, I should feel he meant me any harm, as if the comfort he'd offered me was intended as misdirection for the hurt he was about to inflict upon me. I paused in the dim hallway to breathe, resting my hand against a burgundy painted wall. I was manifesting scenarios in the darkness, allowing my imagination to run wild, the way I had the first night while leaning on the stone wall before falling into my dream.

With the constant reminder floating in my head that I was safe, I drifted barefoot down the staircase ascending into the main foyer of the mansion. The French doors opening to the courtyard were now closed in front of me. It was the first time I realized I had never in my wandering found another entrance in or out of the house nor revisited this one. I hadn't wanted to leave. Not since the moment I had arrived had I worried about anything outside. It hadn't seemed important to tell anyone where I was going, and now at least a week had elapsed.

Standing not far from the marked X, the map said to turn left—which put me facing a total dead end. The wall that I had once imagined as a long hallway leading into a room was now directly in front of me. From the wall, the lined dots creating the path on the map extended through it.

As I got closer, the voice said, "Robe off, boy." He was here, and he could see me. His low and direct tone echoed off the tile floor as if it was coming out of the speakers that had been playing such calming music when I'd arrived. His voice mixed with the dramatic sounds that now played in the music's place. My breathing was getting shallow.

At first, I wanted to respond. I wanted to explain myself and not remove the robe, tell him, "I'm a fancy dish," and hope he'd understand, that he would appreciate my modesty. But this was his house, and I had already decided in exchange for the extravagance I had been given, I would play by his rules. Sliding off my arms, the robe fell to the cold ceramic near my feet in a ball. My shoulders felt cold in the places the harness didn't cover.

I wasn't sure what to do next. It seemed less than sexy that my first words to him since our first interaction would be asking him how he expected me to teleport through a solid wall. Maybe there was some instruction missing, or some wrong turn I'd taken. There was a chance he was watching me stand in front of an actual wall like an idiot who didn't know how to read a map. He was most likely standing behind his camera monitor wondering how he had chosen such a stupid boy.

Sweating with anticipation, I was trembling between the building anxiety inside of me combined with the coolness of the floor against the bare soles of my feet. The chill of the air on my body and my ass out in the open made my nipples firm. I felt a familiar brush upon me. From behind, a body pushed against mine. I didn't move while I allowed him to caress my back, run his fingers around the curve of my ass and thighs. It had been so long since I felt a man's touch, at first my body wanted to recoil. I wanted to pull away. But this was the most I had ever been paid for anything, and I was going to play the part I had been assigned. I wanted him to be the one to finally break me.

His arms were above my head, then something was lowered in front of my face. "Open, boy," he said, his whisper tickling my ear. I opened my mouth to feel something round pass my lips and fix itself behind my teeth, a rubber ball, blocking me from speaking, attached to two straps that he fastened together with care behind my head. Running a hand through my hair then grabbing it hard with force, he pulled my head back toward him.

I could already feel my spit gathering behind the ball, watering at the thought of what it would be like to kiss him. But instead, my mouth was already full, and I knew it would stay that way as long as he wanted.

He pulled both my hands behind me and coated rope was quickly around my wrists, holding them together. Bringing his fingers back to my hair, he used his grasp to move me around as he wished, marching me forward to the table sitting against the wall with the vases full of new flowers. I hadn't noticed they had again been replaced with fresh ones from the gardens in the courtyard, different from the blooms that had been there when I'd arrived.

Above the table was a horizontal mirror just high enough for me to see myself. At the right angle for me to get an unobstructed view of the ball-gag in my mouth, the image of me submitting to this man was reflected back through the darkness. Behind me, with his head a few inches above my own, his large hand full of my hair, was Mr. Usher. Dark eyes and hair, a sinister smirk told me he was happy to finally have me where he wanted me.

"Hello, boy," he said and pulled me back roughly toward his body in a way that made me swell.

CHAPTER TWELVE

"Why do you not want men to touch you?" he asked, holding the whip in front of my face. I was on my knees now in a room so dimly lit I was only able to see what he allowed me to.

There had been a device for the wall under one of the vases on the table. He'd said, "You didn't think to check the credenza," while he pushed the hidden silver button. If I hadn't been gagged already, I may have said, "What the fuck is a credenza?"

"I have a prediction that you need this. I'm glad you've taken the opportunity to relax and enjoy yourself. For what you are about to endure here, I needed your body clean and ready to submit, to be fixed before it could be broken."

He was looking down at me, drool forming around the edges of the sphere in my mouth, my legs spread apart at the knee in front of him. His hair was nearly black and fell effortlessly in place aside from a single strand on his forehead. Mustache and scruffy face, the stubble on his defined chin gave way to a fully buttoned collared shirt. Like his fitted slacks held with a polished belt buckle, everything on his body was tailored and flawless; he was letting me take it all in, allowing me from my kneeling position to get a full view from his eyes to his boots;

both made me feel more naked. It was difficult to understand how a man this attractive would ever pay for sex.

"Someone has to give you permission to be happy, and I'm going to allow you that happiness at a price." He dropped the tip of the whip toward my spread knees. My bare legs opened like the top of an arrow pointing its way to the more delicate parts being cradled inside the pouch of the jockstrap.

His tool was different compared to any sort of whip I'd seen used for sexual purposes, the handle was long and thin with just one single snapping tail. He let the strand dangle near my inner thighs, tracing the sides and lightly hitting them with the tip of the rod. The sting was light at first, but as it continued over the same patches of skin, it developed into a searing pain. Using his polished boot, he kicked my right knee, then my left.

"Wider" he said, and my body fell where he wanted it, my stance now open enough to feel the air finding its way inside the pouch.

Bringing his boot up, he brought it down slowly to rest it on my cock, knowing I was hard inside. He let the rough sole press more firmly, just enough to create discomfort. Then using the tip of his boot gave the underside a light tap. My body shuddered and I winced, the spit I'd been trying so hard to contain behind the ball now flowing in light streams down my chin. I wanted to bring my legs together and fall on my side, allow myself to recover, but I let the discomfort well-up inside me instead. Tears met the spit on my chin.

He laughed, hovering the boot back over my cock, leaving it suspended while his eyes fixed on mine with intensity. At first I was concerned about being sexy, about being this perfect object for his sexual desire. Wet-faced and eyes tightened in strain, I didn't feel desirable. But as he lowered his boot again and pressed down hard, I realized he wasn't paying for my sex at all. This was the game of torment he had to purchase; it was physical and psychological warfare.

"Understand, I can buy anything boy. I won't buy your body, but you will give it to me," he said, finally releasing my cock from under his boot. Walking backward, he put the whip away, trading it for a different instrument I couldn't quite make out in the lack of light.

"Up," he said rubbing the new tool between his hands. It was something thicker than the whip, but still black. With my hands tied, I wasn't certain how I was going to stand without something to grab onto. I could roll over onto the floor and try to wiggle to a standing position, but I wasn't sure that was what he wanted, if it would please him to have me look like a fish on the floor, gasping for air. Some part of me couldn't commit to looking so helpless. So instead, I rocked back quickly, letting my ass touch my heels before using the momentum to thrust myself up on my feet. I nearly fell forward into him but was able to steady myself—which was lucky because he didn't reach out to catch me.

"Alright, on to the bench, face down." He was still holding the object which now that I was closer looked to be made of the same material as the ball-gag, just more cone shaped, with rounded edges. It was black paired with red accents, like most of the decor in the room.

I turned around to face the area he was pointing, moving toward something that looked like a converted weight bench. It welcomed me to squat down and throw my stomach on top, letting my face hang over the front edge. Just behind it, I could see the giant X—the wooden structure I remembered from my dream.

He saw me looking. "The Saint Andrew's Cross, yes. Maybe next time. I have plenty more to show you in here before we get back to that."

With my legs bent at the knees and spread apart with my ass in the air, I knew he had a clear view of my hole. Before I could think much more about what he meant by *back to that*, I could feel his legs pressing against mine, still safely clothed in his pants. The fabric against my skin felt like high-thread sheets. I watched the drool from the gag drip to the cement floor below me.

Chapter Thirteen

He knew I couldn't respond but asked anyway, "What if I opened your hole right now, boy?"

I started to murmur behind the ball-gag, not that I was even certain what I was trying to say.

Pleased enough with my inability to have an opinion of his proposed actions, he continued. "Have I earned your trust, boy? Have I shown you that all I want is your happiness? If I shove this plug in your hole, will that make you happy?"

He was treating me the way he had treated Roderick, letting the toys do the work for him. The clothing, the whips, the restraints. It was all so elaborate that it finally hit me—he was afraid to fuck me. He wasn't going to touch me at all, not with his body, not without something between us. Usher had been telling me I needed him to give me permission to experience pleasure, like he was going to free me from something. But there was a chance he needed me just as much as I needed him. Aside from our tax brackets, perhaps he and I weren't so different at all.

I did my best to push the gag out of my mouth, but it wouldn't budge. Fearing the whip or a swift boot to my balls as punishment, I wiggled my ass anyway to gain momentum. Straightening the bend in my knees, I stood, straddling the bench and attempting to flip myself around. His flat palm was immediately on my back as he growled, "What are you doing, boy?"

Continuing to move, his force was greater than mine, and his hand was soon around my neck, bracing it hard. My air restricted, he continued to push his weight against me to get my body facedown on the bench and returned to position. I lowered my chin to tuck one of the fingers he had near my throat between the strap of the gag and gave a quick tug. The spit-covered ball slipped down my bottom lip, and I wasted no time to say everything I wanted to say, "Please kiss me, give me your cock, let me feel you. Please touch me!" I was begging for everything I had been avoiding for so long.

His hold on my neck and back released, leaving me straddling the bench and still restrained. I didn't move; I was too terrified. I knew I had made a mistake and that at best I was about to be beaten mercilessly. It was too scary to imagine a worse option. For a moment, it was quiet until I could hear the sound of his boots stepping backward slowly on the cement.

"No," he said, "that's not what we do."

"Please, let me see you." I had already gone this far and just wanted to look into his eyes. I wanted to know what he was thinking, to see for sure how badly I had just messed everything up.

His footsteps inched closer to my ass again, and I prepared for the whip. I steadied myself for the large toy he had prepped to be shoved inside of me without warning. Instead, his hands found my wrists and untied the smooth rope. He braced me by the shoulders as he lifted and spun me around. My ass now on the bench and sitting, our eyes met. I wanted him. I needed him. Something was there now, something I hadn't seen before, a sparkle from deep behind his stare as he leaned in close to me.

His lips against mine in that moment would have made me cum where I stood, but instead he pushed me onto my back and unbuckled his pants. My harness pushed into my shoulder blades from the firmness of the bench. The view from my back was limited, but I could see him taking out his cock, feel him edging closer to my hole. He leaned down and over me, our lips close to touching. "Say it again," he said. It was demanding but sincere. I knew exactly what he needed to hear.

"Please," I said, "touch me." His fingers wrapped around the front of the harness, and he pulled it in sync with the moment his cock pushed inside of me. We were intertwined on the bench, his hands occasionally lifting my legs to bury the full-length of himself in my depths. There was raw passion but no subtlety in the motions; we had both waited too long for nuance. He grabbed around my hair, yanking with force as I opened his shirt and wrapped my arms around his back, feeling his sweat from pumping in and out of me, his bare skin against mine.

"Is this what you wanted, boy?" His voice came from somewhere uncontrolled, from a place I could only assume he hadn't let himself go with a boy before. It was pleasure mixed with anger and terror. His palm came down hard and flat across my face, the other occasionally hitting my ass or outer thighs with a smacking sound or a hard tug on my nipples, a pull on my bottom lip, the vulnerability he was experiencing manifesting as pain he had to share. I was happy to take it all, to ride the sensation with him.

His hand eventually landed in my mouth, and I sucked his fingers hard, imagining they were his cock filling my other hole at the same time as it was filling my ass. His eyes were back on mine as he took the spit from my mouth and brought it down past my chest and stomach, reaching the band of the jockstrap and sliding his fingers under. I was so wet between my leaking pre-cum and the spit, I knew it wouldn't take much to get me there.

"Tell me who your cum belongs to," he said.

I didn't hesitate. "You," I said as he pushed himself harder and faster into me. He continued to flick at the head of my dick, stroking it occasionally with force, using the wetness building under the pouch.

"Is your body mine?" I could feel he was just as close as I was.

"Yes!" I yelled into the cement room, my words bouncing from the floor and walls.

"Cum, right now." On his demand, I came on the hand stroking me. The spurts shot hard and fast, coating the inside of the jockstrap. At that same moment, he burst in me, screaming and moaning as the eruptions filled deep into my hole. Our collective sounds mixed with the programmed tones in the red room.

Still within me, he reached his hand from under the jockstrap and up to my mouth. He pushed my own liquid through my lips, and I sucked and swallowed the flavor. I wanted him to pull his cock and let me lick it clean, let me taste us both.

With my legs beginning to relax, I felt him pull out of me. My eyes closed and my head rested on the bench with relief. I wanted to kiss him; if I couldn't have more of his cock then I at least wanted his lips. But the next sound after the moans of our simultaneous climax was a door slamming closed. He hadn't kissed me, even once.

Whatever passion I had raised in him was limited and stopped the moment he released. I was alone in the room, his cum dripping out of me.

Chapter Fourteen

I didn't call after him to stay. Instead, I stayed sprawled on the bench wondering how long I was supposed to wait, whether he'd be coming back or if there was some acceptable amount of time I should stay in position. I lay there long enough for the warmth he had left in me to turn cold in his absence. What had felt like an antidote to my loneliness just moments before felt like poison in me now. I knew I had likely just ruined everything he had built for us by being so insistent, by not playing by his rules.

I needed a bath. Tip-toeing in the darkness, I saw that the lights were already on outside the steel door. The music had been returned to the classical soundtrack, even in the hallway. I took it slowly, still sweaty and wet, my skin and face burning from where his hand had made contact. When I exited through the open space where the wall and table had once been, it slid closed behind me. The vases and flowers remained unbothered. Either the house was smart enough to sense motion or someone was still watching me.

My room had been cleaned, everything turned over and made, satin pajamas laid out on the bed, and a hot bath with flowery bubbles already drawn. My first concern was pulling the damp jockstrap and harness off me; my second was how these people I never saw always seemed to know exactly when and what I needed so precisely. If I hadn't been so sticky, I may have picked up the phone to simply say, "Thank you." Something about knowing they wouldn't respond made me feel empty.

Letting myself disappear under the bubbles, I thought about Usher, about how I had expected him to be a dirty or disfigured old man from the black box of his video chat, that despite his kinks, he was not only handsome but charismatic. We were not so different in age, although he was still a Daddy type. It didn't matter to me either way, but I assumed his hair was naturally more grey than the jet black he presented, that if he allowed it to be natural he'd have a distinguished salt and pepper look. My mouth submerged under the surface, I breathed through my nose and fantasized that if we had met outside of this situation, we could have been something more than a financial exchange.

Suds clinging to my torso when I climbed out of the tub, I could see in the surrounding mirrors that my body was raw and already starting to bruise from our encounter. Even though the warm water had soothed me, he had left my hole sore and well-used. I'd come to associate that feeling with guilt and shame. Not because of the sex, but for letting them have me for so little. This felt different, even if I hadn't experienced passion with Usher, the price tag was finally right. If I could build a tolerance to the more physical portions of our sessions, I could do it for as long as he would have me. Assuming he still would.

A quick knock on the door and another silver tray outside, this time with a grilled sandwich and tomato soup—comfort food, the type of meal Roderick and I would describe to each other after our parents had kicked us out around the same time. When meals like that ended and we were instead eating anything that could be broken open with a can opener in a tent, we'd say, "Remember warm soup?" and feed each other unseasoned beans or mushy spinach with a shared spoon.

The bath and soup helped, and although I still had Usher on my mind, his smile and intensity—I mostly wondered when I would see him again, or if he would leave the house right away. Tucked under satin sheets, I could almost sense him coming into my room, holding me close while he asked how I was feeling, massaging me gently in the places I told him hurt, running his hands through my hair and doing everything he could to heal the wounds he had inflicted on my body for his enjoyment.

But the pleasant thoughts quickly clashed with images of him bending me over hard and fast, hitting me over and over again and forcing any object of his choosing inside me, the impersonal side of his need a constant contrast with the moment we had shared together. A moment I worried we would never have the opportunity to replicate again, nor the chance to smooth it over, to show him that I accepted and craved his vulnerability. That he could kiss me.

Otherwise, I slept soundly for the remainder of the evening and let myself stay in bed the next day. I told myself unless I was summoned, I wouldn't wander. I wouldn't go looking for more information. Three meals came and went, delivered swiftly with extra treats: strawberry truffles and a giant milkshake, raspberry cookies, and dainty cakes. A note with a request for laundry put me in a strange position to set the dirty blue jockstrap outside the door only to have it returned clean and folded on its own silver tray. I assumed it was nothing the workers here hadn't seen before.

I kept my mind occupied with movies and binge-watched everything I could, never knowing when my time could be up, if at some point the next knock on the door was going to be a note telling me to go home, to return to squalor. I was uncertain if I'd done a good enough job pleasing him to secure my placement, if that's what he even wanted, a live-in play toy. Best case scenario, that was what I had become.

CHAPTER FOURTEEN

My anxiety was getting to me again. The thought of having gone too far with Usher always pecked at my brain. I needed something to focus on, a game, like the mindless ones people had on their phones. Usher had bought one for Roderick. If he had given him one, there was a chance I had been good enough to earn one as well.

I picked up the receiver, "Could I get a phone please? Like a cell phone? The kind with games on it?" I heard the breathing and then the click, the sounds I had learned to associate with a request about to be filled. But nothing came. No knock on the door or silver trays, nothing. I hadn't been good enough.

The sadness of my first request being denied stayed with me through the evening and into the next day. I thought about Darius and how I hadn't even told the boys where I was going or left a note. In fairness, I hadn't figured I would be gone for more than a few hours, but here I was over a week later—I had to find a way to tell them I was okay, that I was safe, relatively.

The phone I'd been using to request things had a dial on the front, something I had only seen in old movies, but I understood enough how to work. I put my finger in and spun it to the first number of Darius' cell phone, the only phone number I knew by heart anymore. I finished it, letting each number click back at me one at a time as the dial spun back. Then, nothing, no trilling to assure me it was calling out to anywhere outside the house. I didn't have much experience with landlines, but after hanging up then picking it up again, I should have noticed before there was never a dial tone. This phone was strictly internal for use inside the house only.

My quest for a real phone began in the morning. The sounds of woodwind instruments greeted me as I walked through the wings and floors of the house. My bruises had begun to turn different colors, but most were starting to fade and no longer hurt when I moved. I searched from room to room, finding mostly locked doors but also some spaces I had never seen before, rooms filled with more books and paintings, high-backed velvet furniture and carved boys. Every time I found another fancy phone, I'd pick it up only to hear the same breathing and click. The even breath eventually turned into a sigh, some poor person intended to wait on me undoubtedly exhausted by my relentless mission.

Once, to the sigh, I said, "Please, I'm just trying to call my friend," and the line clicked off immediately. I hadn't been given any rules, and I wasn't doing anything aside from sitting in bed all day getting fat off snacks and watching movies. So I put on a fresh pair of jeans and boots from the wardrobe and took off for the backdoor. If I couldn't call, then I'd just take a walk, a short one to let Darius and the boys know I was alive. Then I'd come right back.

When I reached the double-doors, it was dusk. It had been hard to tell the other night from the inside, but looking through the panes of glass, I could see the doors had been locked from the inside. I turned the locks and pushed. Correction: the doors had been locked from both sides. Chains rattled against the wooden doors and glass. Something large and metal, like the storm shutters my parents had used during hurricanes, blocked the windows and what was left of the daylight from coming through. It was no longer a door. I hadn't thought to check before, but running to every window I had found in the rooms I could access revealed the same metal sheeting over the glass.

I picked up the closest phone. "Am I not allowed to leave? I just want to tell my friend I'm alright." No answer. I was beginning to panic. Out of pure desperation, I tried something else. "Is that you...Sir?" I was still unsure what to call him but didn't dare use his name. The line clicked again, making it clear no one that could help was listening. Of course it wasn't him. He probably wasn't even here anymore. Whoever was keeping me locked inside was just doing their job.

As a last effort, I ran down the stairs and past the locked double-doors. On what I now knew was called a credenza, I lifted the left vase and pushed the silver button below it, the way I had seen Usher do during our night together. The wall slid open like a panel, the long table following with it as a single unit, opening to the long hallway. I walked through slowly, unsure if the wall would close behind me. If it did, I had no idea how to get out. Toward the door, silhouetted in red, the hallway seemed as long as it had in my dream, different somehow than when I had been marched down it by my hair with Usher.

It was the sounds that drew me in closer; the ominous tones coming from behind the door made it impossible to turn back around. Then the screams, the moans, the cracking of a whip and a voice that said, "More, boy. You're going to give me more."

Another crack and scream, then a familiar voice muffled and yelling, "Please, I can't! I'm sorry! I won't do it again!" The voice sounded like Roderick.

Chapter Fifteen

I retreated immediately back down the hallway. This time the panel didn't close behind me, and I had to push the button under the vase to let it slide closed again. I fled back up the stairs and into the east wing, back to the relative safety of my room where I let myself ball under the covers and cry. I don't know how much time went by while I soaked the sheets and blankets with my tears. When I finally took a normal breath again, my face was swollen and wet, and my lips tasted salty.

It was hard to pinpoint the exact reason I was so upset and overwhelmed, why I had let my emotions spill over as if I'd been holding them in forever. I couldn't even remember the last time I had cried. Not when I was living on the street. Not when I was about to get kicked out of my house. Not even when my stomach was so empty it hurt and I didn't know where my next meal was coming from.

Today, maybe it was knowing I was trapped in a house or being in a quasi-relationship I had no control over. This realization that I wasn't the only boy in the house, that I wasn't special, sat like a boulder in the pit of my stomach. To top it off, if my ears hadn't deceived me—if I wasn't just making a bad situation worse to drive myself over the edge—the other boy here was

Roderick. I was crying because I was certain now, at least one man had been lying to me.

Usher didn't ask for me after my tears dried. No notes were paired with the food that arrived at my door. I spent two days staring outside the bedroom window through the small opening in the metal sheeting overlooking the woods and the large trees, the same scenery I had once found so calming. But in my solitude and contemplation, I still couldn't decide that if given the opportunity, I'd even leave.

Lunch arrived, another pressed sandwich with warm soup, something I could have used after spending half a day sobbing into my pillows, but it was better late than not at all. I slipped the tray inside and lifted it to the bed. Picking up the napkin to tuck into my lap, I found something underneath: a phone. A real phone. One with a touch-screen and everything. I unlocked it immediately, expecting it to be disconnected from the outside world. Maybe Usher felt bad enough for leaving me in the room neglected for so long, he was offering me the form of entertainment I had requested.

To my surprise, the numbers made sounds when I pressed them, and when I hit the green button to make the call to Darius, the line trilled. A sleepy voice on the other end said, "Hello?" It was Sonny.

"Sonny! Praise Cher, I need you to put Darius on."

"Did you get locked out?" As usual, he sounded exhausted and three rips deep.

"What? No, I'm not even there, I'm—just give the phone to Darius," I said, knowing it would be less than useful to explain anything that was going on to Sonny. My best chance was to hope he could stay awake long enough to bring the phone to someone who could form sentences.

There was silence, followed by a long yawn, then Sonny yelling, "Darius! Your phone was in the couch cushions again, and Alexander wants to talk to you." Somehow, he seriously had no idea I hadn't been there for almost two weeks. I wish I had the ability to sleep that well.

The change in tone was immediate. "Bitch, where are you?" It was Darius. I felt myself smiling just hearing his voice, but realized right away I didn't know how to answer the question. If I told him everything, he'd want to call the police. Even if I could convince him to come here and help me, I didn't want to put him in danger. Moreso, I wasn't certain yet if I wanted to leave.

"Hello? Are you okay?" he asked again. He sounded genuinely concerned.

"I'm okay," I said, trying to stay calm and contain my excitement.

"So you were just gonna take off and not tell anyone? Are you coming back? Don't think you don't owe rent just because your body isn't in there. All your shit, all that computer equipment and whatever, is still taking up space." He was asking all the right questions, but I couldn't give him the answers. Not yet. Just the image of my old room, the damp smell and chipping paint, the small bed and empty refrigerator, helped me make up my mind quickly. I needed to stay here. I wanted to stay.

"Do you have a pen? I'll get you the rent money and more." On the other end of the phone, there was a sigh. I understood his hesitation, not knowing what kind of bullshit I was about to drag him into.

"Alright girl, go ahead." Darius was a better friend than I gave him credit for. I just hoped I wasn't putting him in a bad situation by giving him the address.

It was uncertain how long it was going to take for him to reach the location, but I made sure the volume was turned off and the phone was set to only vibrate for when he called back to let me know he had arrived. Hours passed, but still nothing. The worry was constant, my mind cycling through the possibility that receiving the phone had been an elaborate trick, Usher testing my submission, that without explicitly telling me I was to have no communication with anyone else, I still should have known.

There was a chance that by calling Darius, I had failed, that at any moment I would be escorted out of the house. Punishment I could take, and at this point, welcomed. If misbehaving would get me closer to him again, if I could somehow get Usher's attention—it would be worth any amount of abuse he felt he needed to inflict upon me as long as I didn't lose my place here, the comfort, the luxury, but more importantly, his affection.

A vibration purred near my head, a familiar number on the screen. "Hello?" I was whispering now, just in case.

"I'm here," Darius said on the other end, "but it's empty."

"What do you mean? Are you sure you went to the right place?" I asked, confused. How could it be empty?

"I went to the address you gave me, but there's no one here. No one lives here anymore." He said this with certainty.

"Did you do the special knock?" It seemed like a stupid question to ask since I had made it so clear during our first call. Three knocks, two knocks, one knock. The system Roderick and I had developed to give the *okay* during a con. Over time it had become a shorthand for so many things. All good, I need you, please help me—it was the audible code of our friendship and the only thing I could offer to Darius to try in case Roderick was on the other side of his apartment door worried Usher was coming to get him for more chastising.

I sent him there with the promise of reimbursement, knowing Roderick had plenty to hand over, and would, for me. I'd already decided I would find a way to pay him back once I figured out how. There was still a chance he had never been here at all, that other than the night we came together, Roderick was not involved with Usher anymore. He could be totally safe with his weird furniture and the money he'd gotten away with. Maybe I'd let myself believe I heard his voice the other night only to hurt my own feelings, the house and the solitude getting to me, making me create stories.

"I did the knock; I even opened the door. When I say empty, I mean EMPTY, girl. There's not a person or teacup in this place. I'm not sure who this friend is, but it looks like they cleared out with whatever money of yours they had with the quickness."

Roderick was gone. Something had happened. There was no way he had left that palace he built for himself on his own. A strange feeling trickled down my neck and my blood rushed.

"So what now?" Darius was still on the other end, waiting for my instruction. As I began to speak, the phone buzzed; it was going to power down. Whoever had given me the phone hadn't provided a way to charge it.

"Go back to the house, sell everything in my room and use it for whatever the boys need." I still didn't know when my time here would be up, if I was setting myself up for disaster when I'd inevitably come home completely penniless. There was a chance that equipment was my only saving grace for when Usher released me, but I couldn't let the boys starve because of my choices.

Before he could reply, the phone was dead. At least Darius knew I was safe. Something about that felt like a win for the day. I hid the useless phone in the back of one of the drawers in the wardrobe behind rolled balls of clean white briefs. Then I let myself bask in the thin slit of sun peeking through the crack in the metal against the window until it faded away and turned to night.

Chapter Sixteen

I heard it first on the door: three knocks, two knocks, one knock. Waking up slowly from the first deep sleep I'd had in days, it seemed early for breakfast. I didn't bother to get dressed since no one was ever outside when I opened the door for the trays. From the lack of light showing through, it seemed like it could still be dark outside.

Naked and kneeling in the hallway in front of my door, I found a single empty glass, upside down, the rim resting in the lush carpet. What a terrible snack. If imagining my drinks was a new game, I wasn't awake enough to appreciate it yet. But I thought of orange juice and iced tea. I didn't typically drink much alcohol but at this point a mimosa or bloody mary seemed necessary.

Maybe it was a message from Usher, his own indirect way of telling me this is where it all stopped, the beginning of the end for the food and fancy drinks. All this cushy stuff, the bubbles and the blankets, was coming to a close. I was right, it had been a test, and I had not done what he wanted. I had called someone on the outside and given him a reason to doubt my commitment to him and this life, our life, together.

It was hard to understand why I was so heartbroken over a man I had only met once, that his hold on me was so strong. I knew I would miss the stuff. Admittedly, the service I'd been aching to provide to him again did just so happen to come paired with surroundings I would never be able to afford on my own. But it wasn't just the payment. It was his eyes, his hands on me. It was thinking I would never see or feel him again, never feel his thickness inside of me. I had wanted the opportunity to make it grow, to let our relationship continue to develop, but now—it was over.

I took the glass inside and stared at it for a while, this crystal symbol of the end. Leaving it on the nightstand, I figured with my stay to be complete at any moment, I may as well use what was left in the bottle of suds, let myself bathe and submerge myself in the grand tub before I was dragged through the house and thrown out in the dirty clothes I had arrived in.

Under the water, I let my mouth blow into the flat surface of the water as I had so many times in the two weeks. I breathed only through my nose in a way that felt close to drowning, the way it feels when the ocean is warm and calm and you're just floating there letting the current take you wherever it decides, contemplating letting go of your control and becoming one with the sea.

Thinking about the vastness of the ocean, about Beachside, I heard it again: three knocks, two knocks, one knock. I let my ears perk up out of the water; it was coming from the other room. Jumping out of the tub, dick-out, I walked in circles around the room attempting to locate the sound. It wasn't coming from the door. Water dripped down my body, soaking the thick carpet below. The knocks were coming from the wardrobe.

Flinging both doors aside, I pushed the hanging clothes and harnesses out of the way and smushed my face to the back panel. The knocking continued in the rhythmic pattern, but it was getting softer, as if the person on the other side of the sound was giving up. But I could hear something else now with my ear so close, a muffled voice. I couldn't make out what they were saying, but I replied anyway, "Don't stop talking. I'm coming! I can't hear you. Hold on!"

Running to the nightstand, my balls bounced lightly against the top of my thighs as I grabbed the empty glass and hopped back to the wardrobe. Pressing the glass to the wall, I finally heard him. "I'm on the other side. Can you hear me?" I could only make out some of the words, but it was Roderick. He was here and he was looking for me.

Pressing my lips as close as I could to the wall and still speak, I said, "I can hear you! I can hear you! You're here! I'm coming out to find you!"

"No!" the voice said back with urgency, loud enough that I could hear it without the glass. I stopped and put the rim back against the wall.

"He's watching us." His voice sounded like he could be trembling on the other side. "Is your friend coming?"

My heart sank. Somehow, he'd snuck me a phone, and I had totally messed it up. I wanted to thank him and to ask him so many things, to tell him about my last two weeks, but with my lips at the back of the wardrobe again, I could feel my breath pushing back toward my face while I simply asked, "Are you safe?"

The glass back on the wall, his response was delayed, probably with disappointment that I hadn't told him that help was on the way. Eventually, his voice returned, "I'm so sorry Alexander, I—"

A loud bang on the other side of the wall silenced Roderick's voice. I whisper-yelled his name to the wall until my lips were flat against the smooth wood of the wardrobe. I moved the glass around to different spots to try to hear what was going on, but nothing. He was gone.

After having drizzled a line and series of spirals around the room in water and soap, I finally grabbed a towel to dry myself off. Roderick had gone through so much trouble just to let me know he was okay, but I didn't understand why he had apologized.

As I pulled the gold chain from the tub and watched the foamy water drain, I wondered if Usher had been watching me since I'd arrived, if he'd seen me pacing in my room and eating cookies naked in bed. Even from outside the house, he seemed to have a way of controlling everything we did, the food I'd been given being the only exception. Roderick had discovered a way to send me messages; I just hadn't been listening. Every sandwich and warm cup of soup, every snack arriving at just the right moment I needed comfort: it was Roderick saying, "I'm here and I love you."

I kept the glass close in case his voice returned, hugging it close against my skin as if it were Roderick, and we were back in that tent, depending on each other. The place we found ourselves in now was so different, and yet it all seemed so familiar. With the glass tucked into my chest, I held it tight knowing sleep would be elusive as thoughts spiralled around my mind.

I'd slept on my fair share of uncomfortable beds or worse, concrete, in the past. Relaxation was impossible in the constantly waking, always in half-dream state that felt like being suspended between two worlds. I never felt truly awake or asleep with the sounds of the city by my ear or roommates grunting from neighboring rooms with thin walls. Here, it had been different. But now, I could feel everything looming. I knew I would be summoned by Usher soon, and for the first time, my fear went deeper than eviction from my new lifestyle.

A hard knock on my door jolted me up. I didn't feel like I had rested, but the sliver of light seemed to be shining through. Still holding the glass with me, the expected note read:

Chapter Sixteen

Mr. Usher requests your presence at dinner.
Your preference for wine is required.

If this was his way of breaking-up with me, it was pretty classy. I wasn't even sure I had a preference for wine. Other than the type that came from a box, with that pink hue that seemed to be the run-off from everything else being bottled, I didn't have much experience. I had to ask myself what Julia Roberts would choose. If she would fill her long-stemmed goblet that was deep but never totally full, with something white or red before tipping it far enough back to take in a generous sip.

I tried to sound certain in my decision when I picked up the phone. "Red," I said without hesitation. Although I was still unsure if the person on the other end was employed or if somehow Usher had orchestrated this entire operation on his own, I knew the time for pleasantries was over.

It seemed clear now that either way, someone had always been watching, that I was being monitored, nothing had been accidental. He had seen me watch movies with my chest covered in cake crumbs and shake my ass in the mirror covered in soapy bubbles. It must have been so amusing to him to see how happy I was in his home. It had occurred to me the only embarrassing thing I hadn't done in the room was jerk-off, which was surprising considering it had been such a ritual before my stay here. In fact, it had been my only form of release for so long and yet, I hadn't even thought about touching myself. I wanted to hate him for keeping me here, for lying to me and doing whatever he had to Roderick, but I couldn't deny how much I still craved him, this wealthy older man who had become my keeper, Mr. Usher.

Chapter Seventeen

T he harness and matching red jockstrap requested in the
next note wasn't comfortable under the fancy suit, but
I imagined there was a chance that was the intention.
I'd never been the type to dress-up, having never really had a
reason. I could remember though, before losing contact with
my family, my mother telling me that a man gets his first real
suit for his wedding. But I figured out at an early age if I did
tell my parents I was attracted to men, more likely my first suit
would be for my own funeral.

Additionally, it was still uncertain to me that today was not
that day. My funeral. At the very least, tonight was most likely
the death of the strangest, but still arguably best, thing that had
ever happened to me. At least I was dressed right for the news.
I supposed his insistence in the second note, that I wear gear
beneath the formal attire, should have been an indication that
he intended to do more than show me my way out tonight, but
I had learned not to take anything at face value in this house.

The new map with a familiar X over a room that had been
paired with the note told me to arrive in the dining room by
nightfall. In my exploration, I'd never found anything resem-
bling an eating space. I had taken every meal in my bedroom,
surrounded by soft pillows and empty silver trays full of food

scraps. This place was as full of secrets as it was rules, and I always felt like I was three steps behind in learning them.

As I followed the map down the stairs and toward a side of the house that had always been a dead end, I found it to be surprisingly open today, another wall turned door that led me to expansive rooms with vaulted ceilings. It wasn't to say the house didn't always look incredibly huge from the exterior, but being inside made the maze feel boundless. The music I'd gotten used to seemed more somber and dark somehow and only got louder as I continued along the dotted line on the map and closer to the giant X. If anything was certain, Usher had a flair for the dramatic. He knew how to set a scene.

He was already seated at one end of a long table when I entered the final room, tapping his fingernail on a wine glass. The globe produced a high-pitched ting sound, a twinkle that reflected off the walls of the massive room. Surrounding the table were too many chairs, at least ten on either side. For a man who seemed to value his privacy so much, I couldn't imagine what sort of twenty-two person dinner parties he was intending to host. It seemed like something only a person with money to burn would do, filling every room in their house with furniture because they could. Not out of necessity, not because they were going to use the house to entertain or crowd it with as many bodies as the space would allow—just because.

"Sit." The sound of his voice replaced the reverberation from the glass. I took my place at the opposite end of the table, closest to the door I had entered from, where a full wine glass had already been set out. The rings of the harness hit the back of the tall wooden chair and prevented me from resting my back entirely. I thought about the bruises he had left on me the last time, how painful they would be right now against the straps and rings he'd instructed me to wear between my skin and the layers making up the suit.

"As expected, you Beachside boys do clean-up nicely." He said it like a compliment, but his tone reminded me of the time the owner of the house I grew-up in came by to tell my parents he was raising their rent, the way he introduced himself by saying, "I'm your Slumlord."

"Thank you," I said immediately, certain my memory was misplaced in this context. He was trying to calm me, to let me know this dinner was just that: dinner. He wanted me here, and I was excited to see him again. Already the moths were back in my stomach and making their way down my abdomen. I had to shift in the chair as I swelled from just the sound of his voice. If I had been upset before, I couldn't remember why now.

"I apologize for my absence during your stay so far. I had business away from here." He paused, looking at the wine in front of me. "Please, drink," he said.

Picking it up by scooping the round part and letting my fingers part around the stem in a V shape, I felt like I was handling the fancy object incorrectly. I watched Usher pick-up his own wine glass by pinching the stem between his index finger and thumb. I followed, using my other hand to brace it as I switched my grip around. He was looking at me adjusting my placement when he smiled and said, "That way the wine doesn't get too warm."

The red liquid was thicker than I remembered the light rose-colored wine I'd had before to be, with a flavor that was rich and sweet enough to lick off my lips while I set the glass back on the dark wooden table. There were candles I hadn't seen at first illuminating the room, large candelabras on either side of us and in one long row down the vibrant red runner on the table. A line of fire leading from me to him as he continued to talk.

"I'm not angry with you. In fact, I'm quite impressed with your devotion. It seems to be in your nature to please."

"I want to please you." The words came out quickly, like a programmed response. I hadn't thought about it, hadn't processed what he was saying. I just knew I needed him to know I wanted to continue to serve him.

"As I'm sure you always have in your line of work," he said, tipping his wine glass back to let the liquid pass his lips. His mustache and scruff seemed lighter than they had before; he was letting the specks of grey I had assumed were there show through. It looked incredibly hot. The half of me that wanted to crawl on top of the table and weave my way through the candles on my hands and knees to sit in his lap and kiss him was fighting against the side of me that knew what he still thought of me—that I was just Beachside trash. I would never be good enough to be more than a toy he hid away, if I was good enough to stay here at all.

I didn't have the words to confront him about the moment we had shared, to tell him that everything he had let go of while we were together that first time, I'd abandoned just as much. I had shed a part of myself I had been holding onto for so long I wasn't sure if it was part of my skin. He'd let himself do the same. I'd felt it between us like a blaze, but only the amount we could both give for now. I wanted to tell him that I still ached for his kiss, that I enjoyed the luxury I had found myself living in at his expense, but that I wasn't just here for the money. I was here for him, even if he didn't believe it, even if that was the reason he had held back and left so suddenly after our connection. That if he was scared, I understood. But I couldn't say any of that.

All of that in my head, instead I asked, "Where do you go?"

"This is not my only estate. I have many houses to fill, boys to meet and train." My gaze on him moved to the flatness of the table, to the dark wood. I pushed my finger at the base of the wine glass, letting my fingernail create its own ting sound. "Did you think it was just you? Silly boy."

Now my face was hot, I didn't dare to look back up. I had always known there was a chance other houses just like this were out there, and I knew now for sure there had been at least one other boy, but hearing him admit it, to say the words so casually, was painful. The moths in my stomach burned like fireballs. I was embarrassed by how much I had given to this man, how I had stayed in the house just longing for his touch and approval without understanding the rules to his games.

"As a matter of fact, this house used to be full of boys. It will be again, soon enough. With your help." I ignored the last part of what he said, concentrating on the fact that there was a reason the Beachside townspeople had created the stories they passed around about this place. They were true. For decades, this house had been used for this purpose. For his boys. According to him, not unlike so many other houses of his around the world that probably had their own legends in the surrounding cities.

I had let myself grow quiet, still avoiding his eyes, concentrating on finishing my wine instead. It was my hope that by the time he demanded I face him, he would pass my red face off as flush from the drink, that he wouldn't know the pain I was feeling in my guts and heart. He filled the air with more information than I expected, about furnishing all the empty rooms I had found, about how gracious he was to let his boys rest in comfort before using them again, why he had to have a variety in order to satisfy him or risk exhausting a boy too quickly.

As he detailed his exploits to me so casually, I suddenly felt bold. I felt angry. Looking him in the face, I asked, "What happened to all the boys that used to be here?"

He seemed surprised by my intrusion on his explanation and paused for just a moment before he spoke. Usher didn't want to think of me as his equal, as someone he could have a real conversation with. "I'm not sure what part of that is your concern."

My eyes lowered back to the table. He was going cold again. The wicks of the candles sizzled and popped. I hadn't noticed before that they were giving off an aroma, more crushed flowers mixed with cut wood, a scent that had become branded to my duration in the house, a priceless perfume without a name.

"It won't happen again." He was answering the question I hadn't asked. But I knew what he was referencing. Our intimacy had scared him. Leaving me for days alone after our encounter with no contact had indeed been a test. Even if he had been away from the house, he watched to see if I would stay, if I wanted him the way he wanted me.

"I will make you happy, boy. I will give you everything you desire. That has been my intention since the first time I saw you. But as much as you will love what I provide for you, I do not ask for nor require your love. Know that I will never love you."

Usher wasn't looking for a boyfriend. There was no need to fulfill in his life that required a toy with more than moving parts. I could want him endlessly, and it would make no difference. My desire was complementary and unnecessary. His words said he needed me to commit to the role he was asking me to play or not be here at all. But my heart still heard the longing in his voice.

"I did mean it when I told you I found you special. When I saw you, stroking that lovely cock on my property, as if you were drawn to me...you knew what I was, what this house could do for you, and you wanted it. Don't ever forget that while I may have instructed Roderick to guide you here, it was you who sought me out, boy."

The words I didn't want to hear, a truth I hadn't allowed myself to even ponder. Roderick had conned me. He had used everything we learned together against his own partner in crime. I wondered what he had been promised in exchange for my imprisonment, if he was in some new apartment with his feet up on his ugly beanbags, drinking his scalding hot tea and enjoying everything he had exchanged for my freedom.

"I have a present for you," Usher said, "or rather a reward. Something I know you're too afraid to ask for yourself. But you must promise me that you will do anything I ask of you from this moment forward."

His gaze burrowing into me, it didn't feel like a choice when I nodded. Smiling in return, he let himself take a long sip before he spoke again, "Your wine is empty. Red, wasn't it?" Usher rang a small bell sitting next to his thick fingers. A swinging door behind his seat opened slowly. Roderick was there, shirtless and holding a silver tray with a full glass decanter balanced in the center. A collar was wrapped around his neck and a leash hung at his bent arm, ready to be commanded and pulled. I noticed his jockstrap first because it matched the one I was instructed to wear this evening. But it was his body, badly bruised and red in certain spots, that held my attention.

I had been angry only seconds before with this idea of him profiting from my misery. But now, I wanted to run to him. I wanted to inspect his skin and make sure he was alright, but I stayed in place and quiet, afraid again.

He didn't speak either as he approached my empty glass and refilled it. I wanted him to look down toward me, even from the corner of his eye just to give me a look that said he was okay. But he didn't dare break his attention from Usher, who watched his every movement as he spoke.

"It's a shame he hasn't had a chance to rest from his punishment which, I'm sure he would agree, was well-deserved. But as I said, tonight, is a reward. I'm going to give you both something you've always desired."

CHAPTER EIGHTEEN

U sher rose and grabbed something from a table near
him, carrying it in our direction. When he was near,
making a triangle with me in my seated position
between each man, he said, "Stand up, boy." I wanted to down
the freshly poured wine first, but I found myself on my feet
before my brain could assess what was happening.

"Undress him." He was talking to Roderick now who set
down his tray and without hesitation obeyed his master. It was
clear to me now that Roderick had been Usher's pet for quite
some time before I had arrived, that he had lived in the house
and had the time to learn far more secrets than I knew.

Our eyes didn't meet as his fingers slowly undid the pearl
buttons of the white shirt that had been issued to me, one of
the garments I'm sure was expensive and fitted perfectly to my
body. His breath was getting shallow, and the first time his skin
brushed mine—his palm, seemingly accidentally, touching my
chest—I wanted to touch him back. I wanted to place my hand
flat near his nipple to see if his heart was beating rapidly in time
with my own.

Usher watched the process, the delicate way Roderick
removed my clothes and folded them on the table, but it was
difficult to say if he was pleased. When I was undressed down

to nothing more than the harness and jockstrap, Usher finally smiled. He lifted my chin, and in a single motion so my eyes were on him, fastened me with a collar matching Roderick's. Grabbing the metal chain acting as a leash, he pulled Roderick closer to us both. Then, using a hook on the bottom end, he attached it to my new collar, a single line now created between us so he could pull us both at once.

"On the ground, boys," he said, tugging at the metal links as we both knelt and found our way further down until our hands were flush with the floor. He walked us back to the other side of the table near his chair where he made us stay on the ground while he poured and finished more wine. There had been no actual food during our meeting and it seemed now, dinner was about to be a very different sort of feast.

There were so many questions I wanted to ask Roderick, with the predominant one being, "What the fuck is even going on right now?" But there was little I could do to make him risk even a non-verbal interaction with me without permission.

As we crawled across the various types of flooring through the house, our knees took a beating from the tile while Usher brought past the French doors to what seemed to be his favorite dungeon. With Usher a few steps ahead, I tried over and over to steal a glance from Roderick, but he remained obedient, and we continued to move forward.

Down the long hallway and into the familiar red light, the ominous tones had begun. It was something I still hadn't figured out, whether Usher had some sort of remote control in his pocket he could access to make it look like a magic trick, or if there was help somewhere in the mansion assisting in the soundtrack to his sexual madness. From an aerial view, if I hadn't been the one with a collar on entering a sex dungeon, the execution and planning of it all would have been impressive. Usher didn't just want submission; he wanted a full sensory experience to be achieved for all participants, and it was.

The door at the end of the hallway closed behind us and locked shut on its own. Taking a half-seated position on one of the taller benches, Usher brought his hand up in a way that made Roderick rise to his knees, instinctively. I followed his lead, in no hurry to disappoint or earn myself the type of punishment that had been so recently inflicted on Roderick's frame.

"Mouth open, boys." There was no hesitation from Roderick to part his mouth wide and welcoming to whatever Usher wanted to put inside. Again, knowing I had agreed to obey his every demand, I followed Roderick's movements. I was being trained by example.

"Are you mine to do with as I want?" Usher asked. Mouth still spread and ready, Roderick forced out, "Yes, Sir."

Usher looked at me, expecting the same. I was uncertain how to form the words without closing my mouth, but using my throat let the sounds of something like "*Ess Sear*" find their way out. He smiled, almost laughing at my need to please, my intention to follow instructions even when they weren't explicitly given.

"Very good," he said and leaned over our still accessible orifices. He pursed his lips and let a droplet of his spit glide out until it landed on Roderick's tongue. It sat there, visible from my peripheral vision where I knelt next to him. Moving a step over closer to me, Usher prepared another full droplet of spit inside his mouth, taking the time to guarantee it would be equal or greater to the previous one. He didn't ask for it, but I kept eye contact with him as the spit fell to my mouth, his taste taking over my own. The wine and saltiness of him sitting on my tongue was as close to kissing him as I had gotten and his saliva mixing with mine was making me rise inside the jockstrap.

"Swallow," he instructed, and Roderick immediately closed his mouth and let Usher's spit run down his throat. This was his way of demonstrating his power, a reminder: he owned us. Our bodies, every part of them, were his. I had yet to close my mouth; Usher looked down at me, commanding my compliance.

More than when he'd asked me before, I felt like this was my first real decision, the moment I would decide if I was giving myself to him, if I would not only be his and stay in this house, but carry out his demands in every way. His spit in my mouth felt like royalty; it felt like freedom from the life I had known before and never going back. I swallowed. My stomach felt full of some part of him now, and I wanted more.

"Now, because you are so fond of each other and have been, for the most part, such good boys," he looked at Roderick while he said *for the most part*. I had come to assume that, although I was still uncertain how he had pulled it off, sneaking me the phone was among the protocols Roderick had violated on my behalf. The signals he'd offered me knowing he was risking punishment, the exact meal I wanted while I was recovering from Usher's abuse, and finding a way to communicate through the wardrobe: they'd all been found out.

It was that level of detail to my needs that had made me leave so long ago, abandon the home we'd created together. The night he had told me he loved me, that he wanted us to be something more than friends sleeping on the ground together, I couldn't be sure if what I felt was more than a codependence we'd formed from necessity. I didn't leave because I didn't love him back; I left because I wasn't certain how to tell if the love was real.

"Kiss," Usher said, still looming over us. "It's okay. You have permission. I'm giving you each other as a gift."

For the first time since I'd left him standing alone in his apartment—told him I couldn't stay for the second time in our lives—Roderick looked into my eyes, deep and passionate, as if he'd been waiting for this moment since the day we met on the beach. Because as many times as we'd gotten this close, we'd never actually kissed. We'd never had sex or touched each other for more than warmth at all.

Usher laughed at our hesitation, seeming to be just as surprised as we were that we had never hooked-up. From what he had gathered by our interaction and concern for each other, I'm sure he was certain we had always been lovers.

"This is not a request," he said, still amused. "Kiss," he repeated. Now that it was an order, there was little to consider and our lips met in the middle. We filled the space Usher had been keeping between us quickly, and his mouth on mine felt like home. It felt like years of longing satiated. My sadness that had felt like deep hunger for so long finally satisfied by the kiss I didn't know I needed, sitting like comfort food and taking over the space I thought I had reserved for Usher in my stomach.

He watched us from the bench for a while, releasing the metal leashes for just a moment while we rolled on the ground together kissing and sucking each other. Our hands firm around each other's cocks, sharing the taste of Usher's spit in our mouths, our collars clinked together as we fiercely caressed each other's bodies.

"Enough," Usher said, quickly done with our show. I didn't want to release my grasp on him or feel Roderick take his skin off mine. Even a few more minutes to feel him inside of me or me inside of him, to continue exploring this place I had forced myself to avoid for so long, was all I needed. But on Usher's command, Roderick released my cock from his hand immediately and was back on his knees in front of him. I followed with less enthusiasm, our cocks both out and hard near his boots.

During our tussle, I hadn't noticed Usher take out his own cock. But now he stroked it slowly and looked at me, then Roderick. It was the first time I had seen it up close, thick and long, bulging through the open fly of his fitted pants. If I couldn't touch Roderick, then I needed Usher in my mouth immediately. I thought about violating orders, about inching closer and taking my tongue to him without permission, to see if he would allow it considering how hard and displayed he was in the moment.

But as I imagined my saliva dripping from the tip of him, he raised his hand up and with a swift motion brought his hand across Roderick's face. The quick smack cracked like thunder against the cement walls and ceiling. Roderick was on his side, heaped on the cold floor, moaning with pain. I was too surprised to move, to check on him, to speak.

Disconnecting the chain line keeping us together, Usher pulled me to my feet by my collar and forced me over the bench he had been sitting on. With my jockstrap still in place, he forced himself inside of my hole. Pulling out just for a second to spit onto my ass, he thrust himself back inside and pumped hard, grabbing my hair.

"Tell me you're only mine," he demanded.

"I'm yours!" I yelled back, knowing Roderick could see everything that was happening from where he lay on the floor. There was pain, but something so confusing within me was incredibly turned on by Usher's inability to follow his own rules, that I somehow had the ability to get more than his whips and toys. I was different, no matter what he said. He did want me.

If I had been drawn to him, he had been just as drawn to me. There could be a million bearded, hairy boys saying they were his in the world, countless houses and furry holes for him to fill, but there was still something we could give each other that no one else had been able to provide.

With Roderick still on the floor, I knew his eyes were fixated, his cheek probably burning with agony while he dealt with the confusion of Usher doing something to me they had never done together. He was going to have more questions for me than I would for him after this night.

Usher came hard and quick inside me, his warmth leaking from the space he had opened so quickly. The silence that followed was telling; he was not proud of the emotion he had let overcome him once again, that he had shown his vulnerability not only to me, but to Roderick. He had put our secret on display, if only to demonstrate to another man offering me affection that they could never have me. I was his.

Pulling backward, Usher withdrew directly, as he had done the first time. I couldn't see Roderick from my position on the bench, but I imagined his shock, the array of emotions he may be experiencing seeing me so willingly claimed. Not moving, I wondered if Usher's cum dripping out made Roderick wonder if I shared the emotion Usher seemed to have for me.

Catching his breath from the quickness and force of his action, I could hear Usher fasten his pants and grab Roderick roughly by his leash, "Back to your room, boy!" he yelled. Then to both of us, "I expect to be thanked for this gift. Make no mistake. You will never touch again without my permission."

I was up on my elbows on the bench now just enough to see Usher dragging Roderick out the door by his collar. He slammed the it behind them, leaving me again laying on my stomach and full of his spit and cum. In the glow of the red light, with his mark inside my body, I wondered if it was the closest thing I would get to his love.

Chapter Nineteen

❦

Through the thin slit between the shutters outside my bedroom window, I could see the trees outside had now fully undressed for winter. I couldn't open the glass or further part the metal on the other side, but if I hadn't been sealed in, I imagined the air would feel refreshingly chilled. Not freezing yet, but cold enough to know a real change was occurring, that the plants outside were dormant only in preparation for their rebirth.

I wasn't surprised I hadn't seen Usher after that night. What did surprise me was my door remaining locked from the exterior unless a silver tray was resting on the carpet. Without fail, once I took whatever was being given to me inside my room, a few moments later I would hear the lock turned again. Usher was keeping me where he wanted me and making it clear, regardless of our intimacy, I did not have his trust.

It took a few days longer than was typical to heal my body from our unexpected three-way encounter, and during that time, I often found myself thinking about Roderick, wondering if the old and new marks Usher had left on him were starting to turn back to his normal shade of skin, if he had been punished further for our lips finally touching, even if it had been at Usher's command.

CHAPTER NINETEEN

After what must have been a week of sunrises and sunsets peeking through the naked canopy of woods, I began to wonder if Roderick was still in the house at all. I found myself often with my ear pressed against the back panel of the wardrobe, moving the empty glass I had stashed away, hoping to hear even a murmur of his voice in one of the corners. Nothing came.

A quick knock on the door and the click of the lock being released, I dropped the glass to retrieve my afternoon meal. Instead, outside on a tray, was a ring of keys. I really would have preferred a sandwich, or anything edible, but I pulled the collection inside letting the metal of the keys scrape as they slid across the surface. The variety of aged blades and teeth were heavy in my hand. Most were long with only a few spokes at the end; it was difficult to imagine the type of locks the odd grooves would fit into. Even with my quick response to open the door, as usual, there was no one in the hallway. The door was finally open, and I was still hungry.

Whether the keys were one of Usher's games or a signal from Roderick, I couldn't be sure. Tossing and catching the keys in my palm, I took them as a sign either way—it was time to leave my room. Perhaps they were a reward, Usher demonstrating to me I had further proven I was worthy and had earned new privileges in the house. Still, more than wanting to secure my home with Usher, I hoped that whatever door the keys opened, I would find Roderick waiting on the other side.

Racing back to the wardrobe, I pushed garments aside looking for something all-occasion. If I was going on an adventure, I wanted to be ready, to have something aside from underwear on for the first time in weeks. Settling on some jeans and boots with a plain t-shirt, something caught my eye behind the now empty hangers. It was hard to believe I hadn't noticed it before, but in the upper left corner where the dark wood met was a lock. As if it had just appeared, pressed in the corner of the back panel of the wardrobe, a strange latch met a loop threaded with a thick padlock and keyhole.

The keys twinkled glamorously around my wrist while I tried each of the strange keys I had been given. Then, success in the form of the lock releasing and the back panel turning into a squeaking door which opened into a large stone passage. Roderick hadn't been talking to me from another room when he'd made contact with me before; this was something else. There were no other doors that I could see, just a cold and drafty tunnel beckoning me to explore. Looking back to the unlatched door of my room, I couldn't be sure this new passage would lead to food, but I took my first step in anyway and let my boot rest on the smooth rock floor.

Beyond the safety of the wardrobe, it was tall enough inside the passage for me to stand in, just barely. Reaching out my hands, I could touch either side with my fingertips without bending my elbows. My breath was now blended with the sound of my wristlet of keys chiming against themselves and echoing from the surrounding stone as I walked further through what became a winding path. The music I'd gotten accustomed to was now silent with no violins or spooky piano vibes penetrating the rock to act as a score to my adventure. While the distance from the artificial light of my room grew, the dimness took over, and I was forced to rely on my sense of touch combined with a slight glow that felt like sunlight and guided me forward. The smell of pine and earth wafted through the chill, and I kept course for the daylight until the stone tunnel ended in what felt like another dead end, like so many in this house.

If I'd learned anything from my stay here, it was that the manor was nothing if not exactly the opposite of what it seemed from the outside. Weeks ago, I would have sat on the ground defeated and hoping I could feel my way back to the safety of my room, but instead I pushed and felt around for latches and buttons, secret things that would reveal the next step. My hands discovered something carved from the stone, a heavy door with a rectangular hole letting the scents and rays find their way inside.

I pushed and slid it aside, and as my eyes adjusted to the new light, I found that this entire time, my room had led straight to my favorite spot on the property. The keys had to be a gift from Usher to show me he had always been watching. Even when I would come to enjoy his woods, I had always belonged to him.

Something glittered from the base of a large tree, one that I had often used during my walks. On the ground, near dried splatters still shining from the dirt, color: blues, purples, and golds. I couldn't believe it until I was holding them in my hands, feeling the grit and sand—shell dollars. I'd always assumed they were gone forever, that when Roderick and I had found ourselves without a home, we'd left behind the last of them. But he had saved them, somehow, all this time and he had brought them here. Like always, he had found a way.

This was a message from Roderick, my first contact with him since the night we'd rolled and kissed on the floor of the red room. The keys had appeared to tell me: he was safe. Out here now, letting the cold winter air penetrate my skin after weeks of being locked indoors, the shells gathered in my hands were a postscript, Roderick's nonverbal message to make sure I knew: even if we couldn't see each other for fear we would be punished worse than ever before, Usher would never break our bond.

Leaning against the tree, the sudden sense of calm and relief was so overwhelming it got me half-hard. The shells slowly dropping to my feet, I imagined Roderick's lips near mine. I stroked over my jeans thinking of the ways I wanted to continue to explore his body, put my tongue on the tip of his cock and lick the underside while I looked into his eyes, flip him over so I could move my tongue to the fur between his ass, but most importantly kiss him hard and cum together. Maybe it was too late. In this world, in this house, we were owned. We'd given our lives and bodies to Usher. They belonged to him, and he had made it known that Roderick and I could never be together in this house.

But outside with the colored shells surrounding my boots, my soles grinding deeper into the dirt as I pulled the hardness from my jeans and began to stroke, I knew Usher did not control my mind or fantasies. Pressed on the tree and ready to shoot toward piles of thick fallen leaves, I could pretend I had told Roderick when he'd asked the first time that I did want to be with him, that we would find our way through anything with our love for each other.

The thought quickly turned to my association with our partnership, the way it was paired with lack and poverty, sleeping on cement in the rain on the nights when I wasn't able to romanticize our very real financial struggle. The truth was, even when the bruises on my body were grey, or purple, or some shade of blackish blue, I was happy: orange happy, yellow happy, shades I could see now that I hadn't been able to before. I was where I wanted to be and felt close to gaining Usher's confidence. Admitting my feelings for Roderick would only complicate my effort to work toward Usher's affection. I had felt it twice now, his resistance to show me the intimacy he craved. Already, Usher had given so many material things I had wanted in my life and assuming they would continue, in exchange, I would give him my body and dedication. I would help him achieve the physical relationship with a man he denied himself.

My cock standing long and thick from the fly of my jeans, pre-cum dripping like an icicle, in my mind, Roderick's presence transformed into Usher. The thought of giving myself so completely, of being a kept boy in such an extravagant household, used to get me hard in the woods. Now, the mysterious man

I'd only heard about in rumors wore the very real face of Usher, and the whisper of his commands for my cum still sent me close to the edge. I was finally on the right side of the iron gates and wanted to stay there. Imagining his breath in my ear again and voice commanding me to shoot, my body convulsed against the rough bark. Spurts fired one after the other as they found their way to the earth, and with my bottom lip under my front teeth and eyes closed tight riding the sensation, a phone rang.

My orgasm nearly ruined, I stumbled quickly to redistribute my weight and let the blood find its way back to my brain. Shoving myself back into my pants, I hastily attempted to fasten the zipper and button, certain I was about to see Usher behind me with a perverse tool, something that could do more than bruise my skin. For this offense, I expected him to draw blood and pull me by my hair back to my room, toss me inside and leave me in confinement for as long as he decided. But, struggling to catch my breath, I looked in every direction around the dense trees and I saw no one.

Among the logs and shrubs close to frozen in the gusts of early winter, it was the first time I noticed my breath visible in front of me. The phone was still ringing. I turned toward the sound and followed it until I was on my knees at the base of a nearby tree not far from where I had just spilled my load. Still bulging and partially unbuttoned, I grabbed up the phone from the base of the trunk where it met the icy ground. It was the same phone Roderick had snuck to me weeks ago. The one that had died, and I'd stashed with my clean underwear. On the display was a familiar phone number scrolling over and over.

"Hello?" I said, putting the phone to my ear. I was still pulsing below my pants with a mix of terror and release, but the former was winning the moment I heard his voice on the other end.

"Where's the door to this place, girl?" Darius asked. I knew I hadn't contacted him or told him to come, but somehow, he was here.

THE END

Leo Sparx

Leo Sparx is a digital artist who is bringing his fascination with the history of queer sex to the literary erotica world. Inspiration for his work is often found during virtual orgies, trips to offbeat museums, or classic—-occasionally spooky—-literature. His unique blend of steamy sensations and dark passion takes the reader on a kinky exploration and allows them to experience encounters in unexpected locations.

instagram.com/authorleosparx

twitter.com/authorleosparx

authorleosparx@gmail.com

More Leo Sparx Books

Claiming Alexander
Taming Alexander
Saving Alexander

4 Horsemen Publications

LGBT

Grayson Ace
(erotica)
How I Got Here
First Year Out of th Closet
You're Only a Top?
You're Only a Bottom?
V.C.Willis
(Fantasy Romance)
The Prince's Priest
The Priest's Assassin
The Assassin's Saint
The Saint's Bloodeater

Erotica

4HorsemenPublications.com

CPSIA information can be obtained
at www.ICGtesting.com
Printed in the USA
BVHW031530130720
583613BV00001B/265

9 781644 501030